The Alpha's Lifeguard Kissed Omega

By
Lorelei M. Hart

Blurb

Fear had ruled over most of my life from fear of the water to my choice of alpha. Now that I'd left him, it was time to face all the facets of life. What I hadn't expected was that my swimming teacher, the lifeguard at a local kids' club would not only be the teacher I needed, but more. Harris might just prove to be the anchor I needed in life.

When I saw Luca, knees wobbling by the pool, I knew something more than a fear of water plagued this omega. My protective instinct kicked in full-time. I needed to know him, keep him safe, share my life with him—and not just in the pool.

Chapter One

Luca Malone

Blowing out a breath, hoping it would give me courage, I picked up my bag and went inside the My Brother, My Sister building in town.

How completely humiliating.

A grown man who doesn't know how to swim.

Maybe David was afraid I'd sprout a tail and swim away from his wrath all those years ago.

I should have.

I saw the sign notating the entrance to the pool area and made my way through the throngs of children, running about their tasks. The place had a modern feel with computers and tablets everywhere, but alongside them books and tons of art supplies. It seemed to be the best of both worlds for a child.

The smell of chlorine hit my senses first, and I backed up against the wall, making sure I was far from the still water that seemed to be endless and bottomless at the same time.

I needed to get the hell out of here and fast.

Scooting along the wall toward the door, I looked like someone caught on the edge of the cliff, I'd bet.

"Hey! You must be Luca. I'm Harris. Nice to meet you."

A hand jutted out in my direction, but both of mine were busy, stuck to the brick walls behind me as though I'd grown spidey powers.

"Um, I'm not sure." My dry mouth could only

push out those words.

I made myself look up to meet the eyes of the sunshiny guy who was so eager to teach me to swim. Silly man, he thought my calling to make an appointment and paying for two months of lessons meant I was actually going to get into those depths.

Heavens above, I was such a loser.

"Sure you are. Come on. Take my hand."

Such sunshine.

"I am actually going to go home. I need to think about this more. You can keep the money."

He chuckled, and my insides turned to mush. "You need to learn how to swim, right?"

I did. Not for any reason in particular. The skill had been denied me in my marriage to David, and so I was pursuing all the things he wouldn't let me accomplish.

The old saying was walk before you run. Someone should've told me learn to swim and be your own person before getting married to an asshole.

Or better yet, just avoid the asshole altogether.

"Need is a strong word. I'd like to learn to swim, but it's not necessary." My words were followed by a giggle. I giggled when I got nervous, and the high-pitched sound became unstoppable.

"Come on. I'll hold your hand, and I promise not to let you drown. We won't even let you get into the pool today, well, not your whole body, anyway."

For some reason, I trusted him. Maybe it was his voice or his unruly curly hair. Maybe it was because he was the one person in the vicinity who could save my life, but either way, I took his hand and let go of the wall.

He led me to a bench where I took off my shirt and he did the same, causing me to gasp at his toned and lean swimmer's body. He didn't wear swim trunks like I did. Instead, he sported those tight, almost biker pants that left nothing to the imagination.

Nothing.

"Today, we are just going to put your feet in and talk about the swimming pool for a while, get you used to the feel of it all."

I didn't budge. Hot body and smooth voice aside, that water might as well have been a clown with an axe for all my fear.

"Luca, come on. I won't let anything happen to you. I swear."

At the sound of my name on his lips, I looked up and saw the sincerity in his eyes. He would save me before I drowned, not help to push me under.

"How did you know my name?" I asked.

"It's right here on my schedule. It is Luca, right?"

Again, my tummy swirled as he said my name. "Yes. So I don't have to get in today?"

He looked over his shoulder at the pool. "Nope. Only your feet today. The rest of your body stays out. Can you do that for me?"

I could think of a lot of things I could do for this alpha, least of all putting my toes in the water.

Chapter Two

Harris Grant

The new pool at My Brother, My Sister was incredible. It was indoor, but had walls of glass panes that could be rolled up on nice days, so it was usable all-year round. I had made a living teaching at the various apartment building pools and private homes, but the opportunity to run the aquatics program here was too good to pass up.

The swim team was due in an hour for their workout, water aerobics after that, but for the moment, the pool was empty, a perfect situation for my sexy but nervous student. He wore Hawaiian-patterned trunks that still had a tag on them, but I wouldn't mention it. He was already too freaked out.

Reaching out, I waited until he put his hand in mine then stepped backward toward the pool. "I'm always especially glad to work with adults who never had the opportunity to learn when they were children," I told him, using soft, encouraging tones. "It shows real strength of character to do this. What made you decide now?"

He'd been moving along, but at my question, he stopped, dropping his eyes. Shit. I was intruding. Often, adults who couldn't swim had some trauma in their childhood, and I was a good swimming teacher but not a qualified therapist. I did know a few to recommend, however, when fear or other emotions prevented a student from accomplishing their goals.

"Hey, forget I asked. Let's go another way. What do you want to know how to do? What is your goal for these lessons?"

He flicked his gaze back up, cheeks flushing an adorable pink. "I thought I might compete in the next Olympics."

Taken aback, I barked out a laugh. "Then we'd better get started. Some of the other kids have a real head start on you." We were moving forward again, and I took advantage of the momentum to guide him to where his toes were at the aqua-tile lip of the swimming pool. "Let's sit down here and talk about how we're going to get you ready to compete with the best athletes in the world. I'm excited!"

He sat, but wrapped his arms around his knees, not one part of him in any danger of getting wet. But that was okay, for now. "Is the water cold?"

I shrugged. "I haven't been in yet today. Why don't you touch it and tell me?"

He did! I had half expected him to demur, but to my pleasure he dipped his fingers into the water and sighed. "Not cold at all."

"So, why don't we dip our feet in and relax a while." I led the way, hanging my legs over the side and swinging them. "You're right, it's very nice."

He narrowed his gaze at me. "About the same temperature as every day?"

Now I flushed. "Pretty much. You going to join me?"

He unfolded those long legs slowly, taking a full minute to dip even a toe, but I was patient. And experienced. Really, at this stage, the client's age didn't matter. What did was creating a positive first experience.

"So...I was thinking that some of your goals might include water safety." I gave him an encouraging smile. "Right?"

"So I don't drown?"

I moved my legs a little in the water, happy to see him copy me. "More to increase your enjoyment of life. For example, say you were at the party I'm going to in a few weeks. My friends have recently installed a pool and invited me to a barbecue and swimming afternoon. If you were invited, what would you do?"

He started to lift his legs but I laid a hand on his thigh.

"You're doing really great. So, would you go to the party?"

He licked his lips, making his full bottom lip shiny and my dick hard. I shifted to try to hide it. "I would go if I couldn't think of a way out of it. If it was, say, a family occasion or something."

"And why would you refuse. Don't you like to visit with friends?"

"Because I'd be afraid everyone would find out I couldn't swim." His voice rose a little, his shoulders tensed. "My four-year-old nephew swims like a fish. And I don't go in at all for fear of stumbling into the deep end and drowning."

"Okay, nobody wants to drown."

"Or die of embarrassment."

And there you had it. I'd seen it a hundred times, more than that even. The shame accompanying the lack of a skill he'd never acquired. "You know there's no need to be embarrassed because you didn't happen to take swimming lessons as a child." He turned his head away, but I cupped his chin in a probably inappropriate move. "No, look at me. You do not know how to swim. But you are doing something about it. You're taking control of your life, and the next time you go to a pool party, you won't feel like this."

He blinked suspiciously shiny eyes. "That would mean a lot."

"You'd probably be surprised at how many of the other people at the party aren't comfortable in the deep end of the pool. But how about I make you a deal?"

"What?"

"In three weeks, if I can get you comfortable enough to get into the shallow end, you'll come to Liam and Edison's party with me." I was telling myself I wasn't asking him for a date, but I really was amazing at lying to myself. "If not, I'll give you two weeks' worth of lessons for free."

"Three weeks?" He was swishing his feet through the water. "You think in three weeks I can swim?"

"No, but in three weeks you will have the confidence to get in the pool and cool off. You won't be ready for the Olympics for a bit longer, but these things take time."

He held out his hand. "You have a deal. So what do we do first?"

"You're already doing it."

Chapter Three

Luca

True to his word, Harris didn't make me go in, or even mention it. What he did mention was a party in three weeks, but I tried not to take the invitation to heart. After all, he was simply giving me some incentive and inviting a friend along, or in my case, an acquaintance.

"I'm home, Atlas," I called out to my best friend and protector. I heard the flapping sound as my lean and large Atlas came barreling in through the back doggie door to greet me. I'd spent all my savings on him, his training, and my new home.

Good thing I'd kept my small trust fund and life insurance a secret while I was married to David, otherwise, I'd probably be six feet under by now.

"Hi, my boy. Time to eat." He followed me to the kitchen where I gave him some food and filled up his bowl with water and ice cubes. He loved to flick them from his bowl with his nose and then play around with them until they melted or he crushed them up. Either way, I had to mop several times a day, but it was worth it to see him happy.

He was the only person I had in the world, which was weird since he wasn't actually a person.

Good thing because I tended to shy away from people in general after David.

I shook my head against the incoming memories

at mentally speaking his name. The psychiatrists said that leaving him was like the worst kind of breakup. They said that one day I would forget to think of him and then one week and so on until he was a faint and distant memory.

It had been three years, and I still thought of him every day.

I took a shower to get the chlorine off me and buckled down to work. I'd convinced David sometime after being married that I could take a medical coding course and work from home; that way he could monitor me and we could bring in some more income. He could even watch the house on the cameras and know that no one was coming in or going out. With my thumb, I checked the tape that covered the camera on my laptop. It still creeped me out that he would make me leave it on so he could see me working as well.

There had been no line as to how far he would go to catch me in some lie.

The thing was, I'd been completely faithful. I'd never strayed even once.

It was never enough.

After six hours of work, I cooked up some burgers outside on the grill along with some veggies. It was still cold yet, but there was nothing I loved more than burgers with a grilled flavor. As I was turning the burgers, I got a call from my dads. They called once a day now that I had laid everything on the line with them about David. Both of them knew something had been up but since I'd lived in a different state, it was hard to know for sure.

"Hello," I answered, knowing there was a smile on

my face. It was the simple pleasures like answering the phone without someone checking the ID first that gave me joy.

"Son, how's it going?" they both said. I was on speaker.

"Good. I'm grilling outside and just finished working. And, um, I did something today."

They made several comments about grilling in the cold as I knew they would but then asked what I had done.

"I, um, signed up for swimming lessons. Went to my first one today."

They gasped but then congratulated me and asked how it went.

"It went great, I guess. I didn't actually get in, but I stuck my toes in and Harris showed me some safety maneuvers so I felt better about it all."

Of course, they were stuck on my new lifeguard. "Harris? Do tell. Trunks or a Speedo?"

I chuckled and thought back. Neither, actually. "Those biking-type shorts. Longer, but just as tight as a Speedo."

My dads made several naughty comments, and I agreed with every single one and then told them about the invitation.

"So, he asked you out already? I like a man who takes charge."

"Dads, it wasn't a date invite. Just a friendly party. Anyway, I'm not looking. Not yet, anyway."

They both sighed. I knew they wanted me to find someone, someone good this time, but in my heart I wasn't quite ready.

Harris was beyond gorgeous and kind. He probably already had a mate.

"Well, don't give up just yet. Oh, by the way, we wanted to come visit soon. In about two weeks and stay for a while?"

I took my burgers off the grill while the phone was cradled on my shoulder. "That would be great. I haven't seen you since Christmas. Come on down, anytime."

We made further plans and then I got off the phone to eat dinner with Atlas, who also got a burger because he could, and I had to keep my security detail happy.

When it was time to go to bed, I checked all of the locks twice and the window latches as well. I turned the alarm system on and off and on again, just to be sure. When I got to bed, the last thing I did was check my security camera app to make sure all the cameras were on and working and then bid Atlas good night as he slept on the floor beside me.

As I closed my eyes, I dreamed of Harris.

Chapter Four

Harris

After Luca's first lesson, I went through the rest of my workday in a fog, although I did manage to focus enough to lifeguard the kids. Of course, it didn't hurt that the swimmers were the team followed by the water aerobics in the shallow end. But by the time the last person headed for the locker room, I needed to do something, so I dove in and swam a couple of miles at a fast pace. Usually that would clear my mind, but as I stood under a hot shower, all I could think of was the date we had in three weeks, and the promise I made him that I could help him get past whatever block was holding him back.

Adults were always a challenge because most people had at least picked up basic skills as a child, even if they'd had no formal lessons. Go to any lake and watch the kids dog-paddle around. What kid doesn't want to swim out to that platform and cannonball off? Or go to a water park and go on the slides? Or said, water ski, paddle board, canoe...kayak...just take a dip and cool off on a hot summer's day.

It always made me hot under the collar when parents allowed their boys and girls to grow up without a skill so vital not only to their self-confidence, but that could potentially save their life. It was irresponsible, and if I ever met Luca's folks, I was going to ask them why.

I waved to Edison on my way out of the center and headed for home where I fixed myself some eggs and toast and watched a series of TV shows I wouldn't remember later. At ten, I went to bed in hopes of falling asleep and making the next day come sooner. The image of my new student danced in my mind and after a couple of hours of lying there staring at the ceiling, I let my fantasies guide my hand under the sheets where it closed around my aching dick. I stroked and squeezed, imagining that I wasn't alone in my king-sized bed but that he lay here next to me, that it was his grip making me harder, his thumb gliding over the swollen head to spread the drop of precum around and help prepare me to take him.

His ass was masked by those ridiculous baggy shorts, but I could imagine it bared, see him on hands and knees there, parting his cheeks to expose his slick, waiting for me, pressing my head to his hole and—

Bam! Cum poured over my fist, puddling on my groin, and finally easing me enough to fall asleep, into dreams of the omega who had walked into my life out of nowhere, and who would be coming back to my pool tomorrow. I might even get him to stand on the steps...

I arrived at the pool early, the next morning, and had time before my daddy-and-baby class to work out again. I tried to swim at least five days a week, but I suspected I'd be doing at least two swims a day for a while. I had a responsibility to teach Luca to swim. And in my mind, I wasn't going to make any kind of move at all until he was at least comfortable enough to trust me not to let him drown. So...three weeks of lessons, then the party, which was circled in red in my mental calendar. Our first date. It would be awesome.

As I patted my torso dry then grabbed for my T-shirt, the dads were trailing in with their little ones. We were halfway through a month-long session, so they all knew the routine and moved to sit on the steps, babies on their laps, ready to continue our confidence-building exercises. The babies were all two and younger, and every one of them could blow bubbles, duck their head underwater, and even kick their feet to propel them a couple of feet from me to their daddy.

All skills my omega lacked. Eep! Did I say that?

Anyway, I wasn't 100 percent sure he lacked the ability to blow bubbles, but his fear factor was so high, I thought that would be the case. I had a usual way of working with adults but these thoughts gave me an idea.

After the daddy-and-me swimmers left I had an hour free, and I decided to use it to write an entire class designed just for my—this omega. If it worked well, I could use at least parts of it with other students.

Of course, their success would not be celebrated with a date.

Just this one.

A few hours later, I was sitting on the edge of the pool when I felt him come into the natatorium...the fancy word we used for our indoor swimming pool room. I stayed where I was, letting him approach me.

"Hi, Harris," he spoke from just behind me. "Nice to see you again."

"I tipped my head back to see him, trying not to let

my increased heart rate make me dizzy. "Nice to see you, too. Grab a seat." I patted the tile next to me invitingly. "I have some ideas to share with you."

"Really?" He settled where I indicated and, without even being asked, plopped his legs into the water. Progress! "What kind of ideas?"

"I've been thinking about how many adults never learn to swim, and if you are up for it, I'd like to use you as a guinea pig for a new program I've designed just for those adults."

"I'm listening." He swished his legs back and forth. "The water is nice today."

"Like usual?" I flashed him a grin, which he returned.

"I think so. Tell me about your plan."

"I laid out lessons for three weeks, each designed to both build confidence and teach new skills. Many of the adults I've worked with find that the lack of this basic skill has fallout in other areas of their lives."

"You mean like where I can't go on a cruise because what if I fall overboard?"

I chuckled. "Well if you fall off a cruise ship you have bigger problems than not knowing the backstroke, but yeah. It is affecting your decision-making."

"Like the pool party." His soft tone washed over me. "I get it."

"So, for today, how about you join me on the stairs and we'll practice walking into the shallow end." I waited for his reaction, watching his expression.

He gave a nod and pushed to his feet then held out a hand to me. "Sounds like a plan."

I let him help me up, trying to ignore the electric shock running up my arm at his touch and thrill at his reaching out to me. "Day one of the rest of your life." *Of our lives.*

"So, about this party. Will we have to bring anything?"

"Just yourself."

"And my water skills."

Chapter Five

Luca

I was still confused as hell. I knew he'd invited me to this party, but I wanted to make sure I knew in what capacity. That day he'd had me wade into the water down the steps to the incline on the side of the pool that allowed me to walk up and down, testing the depths of the water with my feet still on the ground.

I'd gotten tense when some kids came and jumped into the pool alongside us—embarrassed more than anything.

"It's okay. They had to learn once, too. One day you will be carefree like that. You'll see. Focus on the water—your breathing—anything."

Not the water.

Maybe Harris' breathing. I would focus on that.

"How long have you been teaching?" I asked, trying to learn more about this alpha while I was wading.

"Gosh, I've been a lifeguard at summer camp since I was sixteen. Took a class on a whim since I was such a good swimmer and ever since, I've stayed in the water. I try to swim every day. A lot more over the last week, in fact."

I nodded. "Why?"

I'd do anything to distract myself from the fact that I was actually in the pool.

"Let's just say someone new in my life has caused me some pent-up tension. It can only be relieved in a handful of ways."

His hand was on my back, and his thumb rubbed up and down. Probably trying to make me feel better about being a goof. "The friend with the party?"

He chuckled loudly, so loud that the kids in the pool stopped what they were doing and looked over. Great, more attention.

"No, someone new. Someone I've been thinking about a lot lately." Lucky fucking someone. "The thing is, I don't think he knows I have a crush on him."

I shrugged. "You should just tell him. Be brave."

He bit down on his bottom lip. "Like you."

I shrugged with one shoulder. "I guess."

"I think I will tell him. Are you ready to go in more? To your shoulders, maybe?"

The thought of going in that far had my knees shaking beneath the aqua water.

"I'll be right beside you. You can even hold my hand if you need to."

Here I was telling Harris to be brave about the guy he liked and at the same time almost pissing myself thinking about wading in deeper.

"Okay. But slowly."

He nodded, and we walked together down the incline. I looked over Harris' shoulder and saw the kids playing around in the same depths as I was about to go—no one was dying or calling for help. No invisible sharks or massive powerful drains trying to suck them in.

They were simply having a good time.

I could do this.

"A couple more steps. Now, if your body begins to

float, just kick like we practiced earlier. I'm not letting go."

No, he wouldn't let me go.

When the water sloshed against my skin, I almost lost it but closed my eyes and took a few deep breaths.

"Good, Luca. You're really doing well. That's some great kicking work."

I looked down and hadn't even realized I was kicking. Kicking—in the water—that was as close as I'd ever been to swimming before.

"Is now a bad time to make a confession?" Harris asked, looking me dead in the eyes.

I said no, not a bad time at all, needing the distraction from all the almost swimming.

"The guy I've been thinking about is right here, holding my hand. I can't get you out of my mind. And I don't think I can wait three weeks to take you out. How about this Friday?"

That was some distraction.

"Are you serious?" I asked in a faint whisper.

"I am. Unless you don't want to—shit, I never even asked if you had a mate."

"I don't," I said quickly, almost interrupting him.

"Well, that's good. Is that a yes?" He glanced at the clock, and I did the same. My lesson was over.

"That's a yes."

The man absolutely beamed and put both of his fists in the air. Then I realized he'd let go of me, and I began to slosh around and flail my arms in panic.

Nope, not a swimmer yet.

"Hey, omega. I've got you. Nothing is happening. I'm so sorry I let go. I was so excited about dating you.

I'm the worst."

Once I calmed down and Harris got me to where my feet were touching the bottom, I breathed out one last sigh, reached out under the water, and touched his hip. "You are far from the worst, trust me. Pick me up at seven on Friday, or did I freak you out with my um...freak out?"

He shook his head. "Not freaked out at all. I can't wait to see you somewhere other than the pool."

We both laughed at his remark, and now I knew for sure.

This omega had a date.

Not a friend date.

A real date.

Chapter Six

Harris

I'd done it. Mr. Joe-Cool Lifeguard had not been able to chill his jets long enough to get his student comfortable in the water before taking him out to dinner. But as the week went on, I began to believe that my invitation to dinner was not harming Luca's progress at all. In fact, he seemed more focused on me and our clever repartee than on his fears. While I wouldn't recommend romancing all adult students, in this singular, particular case, it was working for us!

I applied my new lesson plans, as well, and by Friday, he had advanced to "floating" on his back with my arms supporting him. He seemed to do best when I was touching him, something I had no objections to whatsoever. "Feeling okay?" I asked, easing one arm from under him for the first time. "Ready to try it on your own?"

"No?" But he chuckled. "I mean yes. If that's what's on today's agenda, I will try it." His grin wobbled. "You haven't drowned me yet."

"Before dinner? We have a date, you know."

He brightened at the words. "I know. But I hope you aren't keeping me alive just for a dinner companion."

The air thickened around us. For once, no kids were free swimming during out lesson. There was a movie on in the main area and popcorn, drawing away our usual audience. "Trust me, omega, I have lots of reasons to want to keep you alive. Most of them don't involve restaurants at all." I'd been planning our first good-night kiss for nearly a week. It would be at his door, where I would then leave, a gentleman, with a promise of another date the next night. I didn't want to rush things. Not with this omega.

"So are you going to let me go?" he asked.

"No, never." As the words slipped from my mouth, I realized what he'd meant...let him float without my arm under him... My cheeks flamed. "I mean, yes, if you're ready."

"No, that's not what you meant." His tone was low, laced with things I couldn't even think about while on duty, yet I was. "Would it be terrible if I asked my lifeguard to kiss me?"

I didn't have to be asked twice. Standing in chest-deep water, I gathered him into my embrace and brought my lips down on his, moving as slowly as I could when I really wanted to pounce. The steam in the air carried his clean masculine musk to my nose as I urged his mouth open and delved inside. He was ready for me and our tongues danced, twining in the first of what I prayed would be many such kisses, and not all in the pool.

Luca linked his arms around my neck and hung there while I kissed him again, and again...and then...

"Ahem."

We froze.

"I hate to interrupt, but the movie ended and the swim team wants to know if they should wait until you're done here." Edison's voice echoed in the natatorium.

"What do we do?" Luca murmured against my lips. "Are you in trouble?"

I shrugged and shifted him to stand at my side. "Hiya."

"Naturally I wondered why they were worried about coming in during your lesson, which should have ended a while ago anyway." His brows furrowed. "So...are you done?"

I couldn't help it. The joy bubbling up inside me was too much to feel the shame I probably should have. "Just getting started."

Edison winced. "Harris, you can't be making out in the pool while the place is full of kids. They will tell their folks."

"It was just a kiss, Edison. I'm sure they have seen their folks do the same thing."

He sat on the edge of the pool, cross-legged, and waved me over. Naturally, my less-than-water-confident omega followed. "I've been watching you two all week."

"I didn't notice," I said, my eyes on Luca.

"Big shock," Edison said. "And I remember what it was like when I met my alpha. It's almost uncontrollable, the desire to touch one another, to 'just kiss' and do so much more. It's normal. It's natural. And it's not something parents send their kids here to observe."

I blew out a long breath, but before I could answer, Luca blurted, "It's my fault. I asked him to kiss me...and he did."

"Yeah, I saw that." Edison was clearly having trouble suppressing a grin, and the swim team, gathered in the doorway was giggling and pushing on each other. "And so did they. Which worries me because at this stage of falling in love, it's hard to stop when you should stop."

"We're not..." Not falling in love? My protest fell off because it would have been a lie. "We're not out of control. But I understand that kissing, at least kissing any more serious than a friendly goodbye kiss—you know, the kind you give Liam every time he stops by—is NSFW."

Now he flushed because Liam and Edison, despite their busy jobs and parenthood, never kissed in a "friendly" way. No, they were famous for embarrassing their offspring with their PDA. "Just cool it in the pool...at least while the doors are open. And if we are closed, don't tell me what you get up to in here, okay? I don't want to know." He pushed to his feet and shook a warning finger at us. "If it happens again, we will refund Luca's remaining lessons. Got it?"

"Yes, sir," we chorused. "Understood, sir." You have to love it when you and your omega are already in such harmony.

"I can't wait to tell Liam about this." He headed out the door, and the swim team kids poured in. "Behave!"

Chapter Seven

Luca

Since after lunch, I'd been a big ole mess. My stomach was in knots, and I'd only pared my choice of ensembles to five, but that was down from ten so I had improved some.

Harris made me nervous.

Not in a David way where I kept the first aid kit handy and ice packs in the freezer nervous, more like my stomach had a thousand bees in it, and when I thought of our date that night, and his lips on mine, and everything about him, I got weak in the knees.

Then, there was the niggling in the back of my head.

Once upon a time, David made me weak in the knees. His kisses were forceful and abrupt, and I thought those were indicators of his passion for me.

They were more like warning signs.

Suddenly, my chest became heavy, and I had to lay my head on my cool desk and force myself to count and breathe just like my psychiatrist had told me to. It helped after a few minutes, but the thoughts lingered.

I would have to be careful.

I had moved too fast, asking him to kiss me.

Maybe this date was a bad idea.

As usual, in my time of stress, I called my dads, hoping they would be home.

"Hello, my boy." James, my omega dad, answered

the phone.

"Hey, Dad." I heard him move around and then the sound of his recliner caught my ears. He'd sat down.

"What's wrong, son?"

I sighed and rubbed my hand over my face. "What if this guy is another David, Dad? I don't have the best senses for these things. He's gentle, and he's an amazing kisser but I'm scared. Fuck, I'm scared to death, Dad."

My dad cleared his throat, and if I was correct, he was on the verge of crying. I didn't blame him. I'd given them years of stress and grief when I was with David.

"Son, David was a mistake. A big one. But I think you know better now—you simply aren't trusting yourself. That damned bastard made you question yourself and your intelligence. What does your gut say? I'm a big fan of gut instincts."

I thought back on the times I'd been with Harris. He was soft and kind. He never rushed me or got angry. His eyes were warm and always sincere. I never worried he would snap or judge if I wasn't ready for something. And his kiss—his lips were tender and loving.

"Harris is my alpha. The real thing. But, then there's my mind..."

He chuckled. "Yeah, sometimes brains suck the fun out of everything. Have you had a date yet?"

"Tonight," I said and felt the heat rise to my cheeks.

"Son, nothing is written in stone. If anything, and

I mean anything, raises your awareness tonight and you think he might be even the slightest like David, then you don't have to go out with him again. And you don't have to continue the lessons. Dad and I can teach you when we come down in a few. Can I ask a very dad favor?"

"Of course, Dad."

"Call me when you get home, unless you are otherwise engaged. Stephen worries about you, even when we talk to you daily. He won't admit it, but the David thing tore him up to shreds. And if you can't call us that night, at least give us a call in the morning—or a text. Let us know you're okay."

Texting my dad after a date was a really silly thing to do, but at the same time, I understood. The things I'd confessed to going through with David had wrecked them.

"I will, Dad. I promise. Hug Dad for me."

We said our goodbyes and after a brief Facetime, he recommended the rust-colored pants along with a navy V-neck sweater for my date. He said the navy brought out my eyes.

I knew for sure they would complement Harris'.

I forced myself to get some work done until six when I ran to the bathroom to shower and get ready. All the time was taken in combing my hair and shaving. I used my best cologne, the one only for special occasions, and put on my clothes, glancing every two minutes at the clock.

He would be here soon and while my dad eased some of my fears, my brain was still winning the war.

I downed a glass of wine right before Harris was

set to be at my house, hoping it would help calm my nerves.

The doorbell rang just as I lowered the glass into the sink and I almost shattered it, dropping it at the sound.

I made myself breathe in and out in a stable fashion while walking to the door.

"Hello," I answered and heard the aloofness in my own voice.

"Hello to you, beautiful. This is for you." He handed me a single pink rose. I took it and asked him in. He waited at my island while I got my wallet and phone and put the rose into a small vase.

"Is something wrong?" he asked. "If this isn't a good day, we can postpone. I don't want to, but we can."

I looked him over. He was drop-dead gorgeous in his button-down shirt and dark-green slacks. His hair was all wild curls, but I could tell he had put some product in, trying to tame it. Those blue eyes melted my heart.

Damn it, I wanted him as much as I was scared of him and how fast he was taking over my heart.

"No," I murmured and forced a smile. "Let's go."

Chapter Eight

Harris

I was not used to being nervous before a date. As an athlete and an alpha, I'd sailed through school in the popular set, dating a lot of omegas, but none seriously. Since that time, I'd pretty well kept up the same routine, casual dates, equally casual sex, until I finally got it that the playboy life was not for me. About a year before, I'd stopped going to the bars, started staying in more playing video games or reading... Because sleeping with people I didn't love was no longer satisfying, if it ever had been.

My dads claimed I was finally growing up, although in my opinion I'd been an adult for years. But they said an alpha wasn't fully there until he was ready to find his omega. Even then, I'd been doubtful. Sure, it worked that way for them. They'd been happily married for over thirty-five years. But things change, I told myself. Modern times and all. Nothing wrong with a single alpha playing the field, sowing wild oats...socializing.

To prove my case, a week before I met Luca, I'd forced myself out to my old favorite bar, one town over, and spent the entire night sitting at a table with friends, never seeing a single omega who I wanted to ask out. I went the next evening, too, with the same result, and went home in a funk.

But the minute Luca walked into my pool area, I became a believer. And when I kissed him, when he asked me to kiss him in the shallow end, well, it was lucky Edison came along or we might have gotten the place shut down. All those omegas I'd kissed...not one made me want to take him home, cook him dinner, and carry him off to my bed. In fact, I'd never taken them home with me, now that I thought about it. We'd either gone to their place or a motel.

I spent two hours cleaning my house before I went to pick up Luca. I tried not to think what that meant, although I knew.

I picked him up and held the car door for him, trying not to let my nerves show. He made casual conversation on the way to The Bistro, the best place for dinner in town, and I answered in monosyllables for fear my voice would give me away. But by the time we parked, all that had changed. His scent filling the car drove out the nerves, replacing them with desire. My cock strained the zipper of my slacks, and my pulse sped up.

"Harris?" Luca's voice held a question. "What would you do?"

Oh awesome! I was so tied up in thinking about my omega, I wasn't listening to him. "I'm sorry," I said, wishing I didn't sound like such a goof. "I got distracted...parking." Because driving my car into the spot was so hard.

"I asked if you thought I should double up on classes so I can make better progress."

"Ah. I think you're doing great. If you need a little more time, we'll just do it." Because I had no intention of ever accepting another penny for teaching him. How could I?

"Okay, just let me know what I owe you then, okay?"

"Sure." *Not a chance.*

I stepped out of the car, sucking in cool evening air and trying to settle down enough to enter the restaurant without having to untuck my shirt to hide my enthusiasm for my omega. Opening the car door, I held out a hand and he took it. And held onto it as he stood. He was a couple of inches shorter than me. Not much, but enough that when I cupped his chin and tilted his face upward, I had to tilt mine downward to meet his parted lips. Hands sliding behind his back, I brought him in for a deep, warm kiss. I could do this forever, just moving my mouth over his and breathing in his scent. Any good the night breeze had done so far as reducing my excitement was rapidly undone.

I shifted so our groins lined up better and pressed into him, giving him no doubt what he did to me. As our tongues twined, he groaned deep in his throat and held onto my shoulders. And then, again. A throat cleared.

"Hello, again."

Luca pulled free and took a step back, but I tucked an arm around his shoulder, shaking my head. "Edison, are you following us?"

Liam, his handsome and successful candy-store owning alpha chuckled. "Our first night out together in a month and you think we'd spend it following you two?" He held out a hand. "Hi. You must be Luca. I've heard a lot about you from Edison."

Luca shook his hand. "Nice to meet you. I hope it's all been good."

"He says you're driving Harris nearly to distraction and are doing well at swimming lessons."

Luca laughed aloud. "Is this true, alpha?" He batted his eyelashes at me. "Distraction?"

I growled, tugging him closer. "I might say it's your omega who is doing that, Liam. Every time I kiss Luca, he shows up to interrupt."

"Well maybe if you two weren't picking all the inappropriate places for kissing." I studied my boss' face, but it held only good humor.

"I am sorry about the pool," I told him, meaning it. "We will control ourselves in the future."

Liam tsked. "It's all we can do to behave and we are fully dressed. Why don't you move the classes until the center closes to the kids?"

Edison groaned. "I can't approve orgies in the pool!"

"I agree. They will have to promise no orgies. But that way if they want to kiss a little, you know, as a reward for improvement in say the backstroke, they can." Liam slipped an arm over his shoulders and drew him in for a mostly appropriate kiss and when they surfaced he grinned. "It hasn't been that long since we were sharing our first kisses."

Edison blinked a few times then nodded. "We'll work something out. Just no orgies!"

"Don't orgies involve more than two people?" Luca asked.

Now we were all laughing and strolling toward the restaurant. We paused at the doors. "I'd ask you to join us," Liam said, "but I have a feeling you don't want any company, am I right?"

He was so right.

Chapter Nine

Luca

It was completely impossible to keep my cool and my wits about me while Harris was around. My smaller brain did all the thinking in his presence. So much so, that the entire dinner went by in a blur. I couldn't even remember what I'd had to drink— something Harris ordered when my words were absent.

"My place?" he asked, presumptuous, yes, but warranted.

"Sure. I don't know if…"

He placed one hand on my thigh as he drove out of the parking lot. "No, I know. No expectations. Well," he chuckled. "There's some expectations in my fantasies, but no pressure. I'm just not ready to let you go yet."

My face heated and so did the tips of my ears. "Dates are weird," I commented.

Harris turned down the radio. "How so?"

"The whole point of dating is so that you can get to know the other person—get a read on them. But the dates do the opposite. You go to the movies where it's impossible to talk. Dinner, you're trying to eat and not be a complete slob and try not to dribble while putting soup in your mouth. I don't even remember what we ate tonight. Dates are…strange."

I looked at Harris as he drove. His jaw clenched and unclenched, and somehow I knew he was mulling things over. I may or may not have semi-ranted about dating, but I didn't mean ours per se.

I'd probably just screwed all the things up.

"Well, I kind of agree with you, though I've never thought about it quite like that before. That's why I'm a big fan of the afterdate."

I laughed. "The afterdate?"

"Yep. I actually don't do this often, but when I meet someone who I really want to get to know better, I make sure the conversation happens. That we can find a place nice and quiet where the masks are off and we can really get to know one another. And here we are. Welcome to my home."

He pulled up in front of a modest but attractive home with a wraparound porch and warm, glowing porch lights. We parked in a garage and he made me wait to open my door again before tugging me by the hand inside.

The scent inside was all Harris. The furnishings were minimal and it suited him. He seemed like a minimal kind of guy.

"I don't like a lot of things around—makes me antsy." He shrugged, almost apologizing.

"Less to clean," I commented. "A cluttered house is a cluttered mind."

"Very true, omega. Coffee? Tea? Whisky?" he said with a gleam in his eye. He waggled his fingers like a magician ready to put on an act at my response.

"Hot tea, please. Chamomile, if you have it."

He nodded. "Still nervous around me?" I watched as he floated around the kitchen like a pro, filling up the kettle and then putting it on to boil before getting down cups and pulling out a neat wooden tea box, every tea organized by flavor inside.

"Yes."

He put his palms out on the marble-topped island and leaned down. "What can I do to help you with that?"

I shrugged. "It's me. It's not you."

He sighed, long and heavy. "What did he do to you?"

I took two steps back and gasped. "How did you know?"

The kettle screamed out, and he turned to take it off the burner before shrugging. "I didn't until now. It was a guess—a hunch. You weren't very comfortable when I first touched you in the pool. You have a few scars here and there. You're back and forth on being comfortable around me. My uncle was abused by his mate. He lived with us for a while after he left the alpha."

All of the sudden I knew why the afterdate was so fucking important.

"His name was David. I should've seen the signs."

Harris poured two cups of hot water and added tea bags to both. "And that's what you're looking for in me."

It wasn't a question.

"Yes. I'm sorry."

He gave me a soft smile. "Don't be. You can hunt all you want, omega. I'd never hurt you."

"I'm still..."

He held up his hand. "That's okay. Just like swimming, we'll take it one lesson at a time—or date as it were. Can I ask again?"

I felt my eyebrows bunch in confusion. "Ask what?"

"What did he do to you? Come—sit. For you and for me, Luca, we need to get through this. I can't be the alpha you need unless... Just talk to me, please. Trust me?"

Gods help me, I did trust this man. I shouldn't, and my mind told me not to, but my heart was a complete goner.

"It started out small, I guess," I said, sitting on the stool beside him and stirring several teaspoons of sugar into my tea. "He would pick me up for a date and ask me to change clothes—into something better or whatever. Then it progressed to checking my phone and my messages. The first time I told him it was over, he grabbed me by the arm and spat in my face. But then he cried and apologized and blamed it on life or stress or money problems or whatever. Months later, he was living in my house, wasn't working anymore. Anything would set him off. I..." The shudder reliving the memories couldn't be contained. I was so deep inside them that when Harris put his arm around me to comfort me, I let out a little squeal and jumped. "Sorry..."

"Don't be sorry. Come here," Harris murmured and waited, arms open for me. I hesitated and then let myself believe. Harris was good. Harris wouldn't hurt me.

He was my true and real alpha.

I leaned against his chest, and his arms comforted me while his words washed over my soul and became a balm for far too many wounds.

Chapter Ten

Harris

I did comfort him. I held Luca close while I planned the death of his ex. No quick end for the man who'd caused so much harm to my omega. Because he was mine, every moment in his company made me more sure of that. And as I gave him a cup of soothing tea and found some cookies in the cupboard to set beside it, I was torn between that anger toward that other alpha and joy at finding my other half.

"Let's take our tea in the living room. I can build a fire," I offered, loading his cup and one for me as well as the cookies onto a tray. "Sound good?"

"Sounds very good," he said, and followed me into the next room. "I'm so jealous you have a fireplace."

"It was a big reason why I liked this place. Basically, I am an outdoor guy, love the sun and of course the water, but when the weather is cold, I just want to be warm and cozy and maybe hibernate a little." I flashed him a grin as I set the tray on the coffee table. "You get me?"

I placed a couple of logs in the fireplace and went about getting the flames going, wanting more than anything to help my omega heal. I'd brought him back here for an intimate conversation, but, if I was honest with myself, I wouldn't say no to taking our swimming pool kiss to its natural conclusion. But Luca had been hurt so much, how could I make a move? No, although alphas traditionally led the way into the bedroom, I was not going to do it. I'd keep it in my pants and let Luca let me know in no uncertain terms when he was ready for more.

Dammit.

Being a gentleman might kill me. I didn't think jacking off in the shower was going to hold me long.

"Harris?" The soft voice from behind me caressed my skin. "Are you going to seduce me?"

I gritted my teeth. How to respond to that? Swallowing hard, I modulated my tone. "I don't know, omega. Did you want me to?"

"Yes."

Every drop of blood rushed to my cock. Squatting in front of the hearth, I was afraid the tip would rip through my pants and get burned. The thought helped to slow me down. "All right, then," I replied. "If you want me to." Rising, I smoothed my slacks down my calves.

Luca's lower lip was thrust out. "Hey, don't strain yourself." Then his gaze focused lower. "Oh...never mind."

When I moved in, I'd bought a fluffy white sheepskin rug and laid it in front of the fireplace with some vague idea about making love there. But since I'd never brought a conquest home, nobody had lain there under me yet. As if I'd been waiting for him. "Just get over here, Luca. I want you on your back, naked before I count to ten."

I got to seven. While stripping.

Luca lay on that rug, the firelight flickering off his skin, and I dropped to my knees next to him. I started to ask if he was sure, but then realized I was overthinking. Not what I wanted to do just now. And certainly not something I'd ever done before when alone and naked with an omega.

But it had never mattered so much. My entire body thrummed with a rhythm I'd never felt before. I took in the vision before me. Light hair on his arms and legs and chest echoed the thicker matt in his groin surrounding his hard, smooth cock. My mouth watered at the sight. "You're beautiful, omega," I said, lying next to him and drawing him close to me. Our lips met, the passion of our first kiss echoed in this one. But now we didn't even have swimming trunks between us, no kids about to burst in and interrupt.

I suppressed once again my urge to rush things, reminding myself that this was the first time for us, that we'd have many more if I had anything to say about it, but that it should be something we'd both remember forever.

My soft kiss choked off in a gasp when Luca's hand closed around my dick and squeezed.

"Omega," I cajoled. "If you keep that up, things are going to move faster than either one of us wants."

He winked at me. "Can't we go fast now, and then slow down next time?" He stroked me, dropping down to caress my sac. "Because I've waited for you all my life. I don't want to wait any longer."

A growl roared up from my chest and I pinned him on his back, finding him slick and ready for me. "I've been waiting for you, too." With speed completely unplanned, I plunged inside him, his tight channel embracing my cock, my balls slapping his ass with each thrust. I clasped his ankles, pushing his legs back toward his chest and withdrew then drove in again. And again.

Lucas writhed underneath me, and I released one of his legs to work his dick until with a moan, he spilled his semen, splattering both our bellies. I poured mine into his body, cementing a connection between us.

When I fell to the rug and gathered him close, I felt a satisfaction unlike any other encounter.

This was how it was supposed to be.

I knew that now.

Chapter Eleven

Luca

I woke up hours later, still in the warm and loving embrace of my alpha. Yes, I was sure then. It wasn't the sex that made it so, it was the way he touched me—the way he tried to comfort me.

The way I felt safe when we were close, instead of pondering all the ways I could get away.

"Spend the night," he whispered in my ear, still behind me, holding on as though I were his anchor when obviously the opposite was true.

I turned around, making sure not to untangle myself, and faced him. "Do you want me to?" I asked, my gaze firmly on his lips.

"I very much want you to, omega mine." He grasped my hip and dragged me closer, leaving not an inch between us. I hooked my leg over his legs and nestled my face into his chest.

"I don't want to leave."

He chuckled and kissed my hair. "Good. But let's go to bed. I'd love nothing more than to take a hot shower and then tuck us into bed."

"That sounds amazing. Let's go." We got up and showered together. I yawned so much in the warm spray that it bordered on embarrassing.

"Let's get you to bed," he said, chuckling. We toweled off and Harris pulled back the covers and let me in before getting in next to me and assuming our earlier position. But then, as I lay in his bed, I couldn't get to sleep.

"What's your favorite color?" I asked, out of the blue, so to speak.

"Oh, more of the afterdate stuff. I love it. Green. And you?"

I felt my face heat. "Lately, blue. Like the gorgeous blue of your eyes."

Harris kissed my neck. "When is your birthday?"

I chuckled at how little we knew about each other, yet, at the same time, were connected on a deeper level.

"Actually, it's next week. Friday."

He gasped and kissed my back. "I can't wait to celebrate you. Mine is Christmas day, for the record."

I snuggled in closer. "It will be a great Christmas this year. Um, right?"

I realized that I'd made an assumption about us still being together during Christmas.

Harris cleared his throat. "I'm hoping to be with you from now on, Christmas, Easter, every day in the future. Is that too much too soon?"

It absolutely was not too much too soon. And my mind had finally caught up to my heart. Harris was nothing like David.

"No. It's not too much, but, Harris?"

He made a noise.

"Don't break my heart, okay? It's a bit fragile."

He squeezed me tighter and brushed my hair from my face. "I promise, omega. Your heart is safe in my hands."

I relaxed and fell asleep with those words echoing

in my mind.

The alarm blared in my ears the next morning and in my waking-up stupor, I reached for it.

Except I wasn't in my room.

I rolled over toward the noise and slapped at whatever monster was making it. "I got it," I heard Harris say.

Something unintelligent came out of my mouth, and he chuckled. "Good morning, sleepyhead. He lay next to me and put his head on my stomach.

"Good morning," I managed to get out after clearing my throat.

"I made us breakfast. When the alarm went off, I was coming to wake you. It's almost ten."

My eyes flew open. "Ten?"

"Yes. You were sleeping so well, I couldn't wake you earlier. You looked so damned peaceful."

Probably because it was the first real night's sleep I'd had in decades.

"Thank you. Am I... You must have things to do." I started to get up, but his look made me stop.

"Oh, no you don't. I don't have a lesson until noon. I'm feeding you."

I couldn't do anything but obey looking into his deep-blue eyes. "Okay."

He got up and held out his hand to help me. "Pancakes, blueberry compote, and turkey bacon. I hope that's okay."

Sounded healthy, but that was how my alpha kept his beautiful lean body. "Sounds good."

"There's some shorts and things you can borrow in my dresser. Or you can come down naked, that's also very acceptable. I washed your clothes for you, but they are still in the dryer."

My mouth must've been wide open because he hooked his finger under my chin and closed it. "Come to the kitchen when you're ready, love."

He called me love.

And I already loved him.

I did grab a pair of boxers and a sweatshirt from his dresser and went to the kitchen. The island was set like a table with plates, silverware, and napkins along with two steaming cups of coffee.

Mine already had sugar and cream in it.

I watched him plating pancakes and other yummy-looking things. "I figured you liked your coffee like your tea. I can make another if that's not right."

I sat on the stool and took a sip. It was perfection. "It's great. Thank you. No one has ever made me breakfast." I was sure not to say, "David never made me breakfast."

"What a shame. This is one of the best ways to show someone you care—deeply." He came over and put a plate in front of me and kissed my temple. "Eat up. You have lessons today."

Chapter Twelve

Harris

He did indeed have a lesson, and we were so proud of ourselves for not making out in the pool during his lesson, I pulled him into the cleaning supply closet for a reward kiss that turned into...well, more than a kiss and less than anything that could have gotten us arrested if someone had come for a vacuum cleaner or bottle of window cleaner.

It was romantic, but everything with my omega was. And hot...the scent of Pine Sol suddenly became an aphrodisiac. But then what wasn't with Luca in my arms? When we emerged, the lights were out and everyone had left. So I took him back into the pool, just the two of us, and gave him a private lesson. The rewards were kisses and hugs, maybe an illicit grope or two, but before things got too crazy we dried off and went home.

Home to my place, after a stop at his for toiletries and a change of clothes. I wasn't ready to let go of him, yet, maybe not ever. But even though he seemed very happy to cuddle in my arms, as I lay in bed that night, planning our life together, I was also very aware of the fact he'd been through a lot.

As a lifeguard, I didn't have a history of dealing with the PTSD that abuse left behind in its victims, but since I'd been at the center, I'd learned a lot. My Brother, My Sister served many kids in the community. Some came from happy homes, others from the furthest thing from happiness. The local children's department placed many of its charges in our programs. Some were in foster homes, others in a local group home waiting for an opening. And I'd overheard enough at my desk in the admin office to break my heart.

These little splashing people, laughing and crying, learning a skill that could potentially save their lives, and that was a major confidence building, well, some of them had been through a lot. My life...I'd been so lucky I realized now, but growing up, my dads were just my dads. Their kindness, support, and when necessary, discipline something I accepted as the status quo.

Trunks and bathing suits didn't hide much, and before coming on staff, I'd taken a series of online classes and one in-person workshop about my responsibilities for reporting signs of child abuse, and how to work with kids who'd been through traumatic experiences. Tonight, as my omega moaned in his sleep, his eyelids flickering rapidly in REM sleep, I wondered what he dreamed. Whether he was reliving the pain inflicted by "David" who'd not appreciated the love of a good omega. Luca had not gone into a lot of detail, but I gathered it was both physical and emotional abuse.

I'd suggested, as we drove home, that he consider criminal charges, but he shut me down, and I let it drop. For now.

"Harris," he groaned, thrashing against me. "Yes, please, more."

Well, there you go. I grinned as I adjusted my hold

on him to prevent a flying elbow from hitting me in the stomach again. At least these dreams I could help come true. Making a quick decision, I kissed him awake and proceeded to show him how happy I was to have him in my bed.

We slept...some, but as early sunshine crept through the window, I woke to find Luca lying between my legs, his hand fisted around my morning wood. "Good morning, omega," I said, smiling brighter than the sunshine. "What are you up to?"

His grin matched mine before those full, sensual lips moved into a pout. "Caught in the act." He shrugged. "Can't blame an omega for trying."

Playful...he did playful so well and after lying awake worrying about him, he couldn't have done anything to lift my spirits higher. "And what"—I asked in my sternest alpha voice —"exactly were you trying to do?"

Luca's eyes twinkled. "I ummm. I can show you?" He cast his gaze down toward the prize in his hand. "That is, if it's all right, Mr. Alpha, sir."

I started this conversation hard, now my cock vibrated in time with my pounding heartbeat. But, in the spirit of the game, I kept it serious...sort of. "I see." I paused, pretending to consider his request. "I suppose it's all right." The regal wave I gave might have been too much. But what the hell.

He licked his lips and parted them before extending the tip of his tongue to lap at the crystal droplet of precum on the tip of my throbbing dick. Then lifted his face toward me, as if in question.

I couldn't play anymore. Hell, I couldn't breathe.

"Do it," I gritted out. "Before my head explodes."

"Which one?" he sassed.

I growled and gripped the back of his head, forcing him back to my cock, not that he seemed to mind. By the time his lips brushed my dick, they were wide open and he took me all the way into his throat. Dear god, this omega would be the death of me.

I watched his head bob as he worked me like nobody ever had...and nobody else ever would again. He'd ruined me for anyone else. A brief thought flickered past—did all alphas who found their mate feel this way? But did it matter? It did work this way for us. And as I rode the waves of pleasure higher and higher, I prayed we'd always be together, we'd be up to the challenges that any relationship brought.

That we'd share many years just like this. My cum boiled up from my balls and poured down his throat, but not emptying me, leaving me fuller of heart and mind and body.

And spirit.

Tears spilled from my eyes and I wiped them away. Because I had no explanation, just overwhelming love for the man the universe had sent my way. And vowed to be worthy of that honor.

Chapter Thirteen

Luca

We'd been dating or whatever it was called when two people couldn't stand to be apart from each other for a little over two weeks. Harris was everything I never knew I could have.

"My dads are coming into town tonight," I said as we cuddled on his couch after a day of being apart—real life and work and all that.

"Oh? So, you have to go home." He didn't sound pleased and neither was I, but I loved to know that he would miss me.

"I do. Do you want to come with me? Stay at my place for a change?"

He chuckled and kissed my hair. "But I couldn't guarantee to keep my hands off you."

"You could come over just to meet them."

Harris sat up and took my hands in his. "Are you asking me to meet your parents, sweetheart?"

I nodded. In some ways my bravery had increased with Harris around, but in other ways, I was still the same person, afraid of my own shadow.

Or that he would leave me.

And I would be alone again.

"All you had to do was ask, Luca. I'd be honored. You know what I'm going to tell them?"

I shook my head no, my tongue still not doing its job.

He pulled me onto his lap so that I was straddling

his hips. "I will tell them that I'm the luckiest man alive to have found you. Then they will gasp and smile. Afterward, I will say that my life is so much richer because of your presence, and I couldn't have picked a better omega to fall in love with."

Over the past weeks, I'd cried so much, some in private and some tears right there in front of Harris. I cried in private for the years I'd wasted on David. Fully mourning that part of my life seemed to be over, but finding Harris had opened some wounds, in a good way. I had to forgive myself for some things before I could let my heart be taken over by this exquisite man.

And right in that moment, I cried for his beautiful words and the fact that I knew they were nothing but truth.

He loved me. And I certainly loved him.

I tried to lighten the moment. "You picked me. Is that right?" I laughed and tried to wipe away my tears, all casual-like.

"It is right. So, you're gonna leave me hanging?" he pouted.

"No, I intend to put this to good use," I replied, rocking my hips against his.

"What I meant, Luca, is that I just told you that I loved you and you have yet to reply, which doesn't sting much since I already know how you feel."

So full of himself, and rightfully so.

"Well, since you know, why don't you tell me?"

He chuckled and unbuttoned my shirt. "You love me. Not like regular love. It's as though I've completely overtaken your heart and soul. It's because I'm so incredibly attractive and loyal and honest. Plus, I'm good in the sack. You can't help yourself. I really gave you no choice."

This man and his cheekiness. It never failed.

I sighed and let my shoulders slump. "It's true, you are good in bed."

He scoffed and opened my shirt fully and grazed his thumbs over my nipples. "Tell me, omega. No more playing around. I need to hear the words from your mouth."

I took off my shirt and reveled in the feel of his hands trailing down my abs. "I do love you, Harris, more than I ever thought possible."

"Oh, my good omega. I've waited to hear those words."

I chuckled and nipped at his bottom lip. "For two whole weeks."

He reached for my hips and pulled me closer. "No, Luca, I feel like I've been waiting my whole life to hear those words from you. I just didn't know it."

My phone buzzed in my back pocket at the moment I was bending down to kiss him and start up a round of afternoon loving. "It's my fathers," I said and swiped the green button to answer it.

"Hello?"

I listened on, watching Harris tease me by pinching his own nipples and unzipping his pants. They said something about being on their way—yeah, something like that.

"Okay. Just text me when you are about twenty minutes out," I whispered, unable to gather the breath to speak louder while Harris pulled his cock from his jeans and pumped it up and down, staring at me the whole time.

He loved to tease me, and I loved to be teased. It was so different to have fun in the bedroom instead of being manipulated into sex.

They said something else and then hung up. I had no idea what.

"You couldn't wait for me to get off the phone?" I asked, throwing the damned thing on the couch.

"Nope. Why don't you take off those clothes?"

I stood and took my time shucking my pants and got a gasp from him when he realized I had nothing on underneath. My dick jutted out, and I mimicked his movements. Harris scooted forward on the couch and pulled me toward him, taking me wholly in his mouth.

I grasped handfuls of his hair and tugged him in a pace that made me want to come in seconds.

He pulled off me with a pop and wiped his mouth. "Turn around, omega, and sit on my lap."

Chapter Fourteen

Harris

And laptime with my omega was why we were half an hour late to meet his dads when they arrived at his home. He did mention they had a key, so at least we didn't leave them waiting outside. As we pulled in the driveway, parking behind a two-seater sports car, Luca muttered, "They're going to take one look at us and know."

I turned off the engine and faced him. "Are you ashamed of me?"

Only half-serious, I was shocked to see his cheeks pale and lower lip tremble. Dear god. "Luca? You aren't, are you?"

He shook his head. "No of course not, but they have been known to be terrible teases and will never just look the other way."

"Mmm hmm." Hand on the door, ready to climb out, I thought a moment. "My dads would never say a word. They like to pretend they only had sex to have me...forgetting my room shared a common wall with theirs."

Despite himself, my omega grinned. "I was grateful every day from the time I was about ten that my room was on the opposite side of the house from theirs. Just their PDA...well, you'll see it." He rolled his eyes. "Everyone does."

On that note we headed inside.

"Son!" A tall, dark-haired man appeared in the

kitchen doorway. "You haven't eaten yet, have you?"

The blond who peeked around his shoulder was just as tall with twinkling blue eyes. "I sure hope not. We brought dinner." Then they both disappeared for a moment, leaving us looking at one another.

"Umm, do you think they noticed me?" I asked, a little taken aback. "I mean...they can't have missed me, can they?"

Luca chuckled. "Give them a second. They'll be right back." Turned out he was right. Not two minutes later, his dads appeared again, one carrying a tray with a pitcher of lemonade and a bottle of vodka and some glasses, the other a platter of crackers, cheeses, grapes, sliced apples, and olives. We trailed after them to the living room where they arranged all the goodies on the coffee table and plopped down in the middle of the couch, sitting so close together not a gnat could have gotten between them.

"Okay, sit down, and let's get to know one another." The dark-haired dad nodded to his husband. "This is Stephen, I'm James...and I assume you're Harris, the hot lifeguard who is teaching our son how not to drown?"

"That's right." And since he'd touched on something that had been on my mind since the day I met Luca and only growing as my affection for him did, I dispelled with the niceties and asked, "So, how is it he never learned this very basic and important skill as a kid?"

I thought that could have gone one of two ways...like, either they would take offense or be sorry for their neglect of their son. The sparkle in both their eyes, the slow smile stretching their mouths...that I never saw coming.

James winked. "Now that's a story, isn't it, Stephen?"

"It is for sure. And we wouldn't have brought it up ourselves..."

"No, please no," muttered Luca, sinking into one of the upholstered chairs facing the couch. "Why?"

"Because your alpha asked." I tried not to preen that his dad Stephen already called me that. "James tells it best though."

"Why don't you guys eat something?" But their son's pleas fell on deaf ears as the two older men prepared to tell a story it was clear they'd shared many times before.

"Later, Son." James crossed his leg over his other knee and drew a deep breath. "When Luca was about four years old, we decided it was time for his first swimming lesson We signed him up at the local parks and rec, you know, for a daddy-and-me sort of class. Stephen was off from teaching for the summer, so he could attend every day."

"Don't forget," his partner chimed in, "you took all your vacation in half-day increments so you could go."

"I did indeed. So, the first day we dressed him in his trunks and a T-shirt."

"And those cute little sandals, remember?" Stephen added helpfully. "And sunscreen, lots of sunscreen."

"Are you going to let me tell this?" But it was said with no rancor and Stephen waved him on. "All right so we piled into the car and drove to the pool. It was a sunny, warm day in July, and we were so excited. Really enjoying being dads, so proud of our little guy."

"We were sure he'd be at the head of the class...okay I'll hush." Stephen linked their hands though, and rested his head on James' shoulder. "Go on."

"Trying!" James dropped a kiss on his partner's head and continued. "We walked out on the deck and coated him with another layer of sunscreen then the teacher announced everyone should sit on the edge of the pool and dangle their feet." He paused and I flicked a glance at Luca who appeared to be grinding his teeth.

"So what happened?" I finally asked. "Did you dangle?"

"No," Luca gritted out. "I never dangled."

James' Cheshire cat grin stretched so wide. "No, he did not dangle. He ran."

"Loops around the pool," Stephen put in, apparently forgetting his promise not to interrupt.

"Right." James was back in the conversation. "With both of us chasing him and the staff yelling, 'No running by the pool.'"

Luca whimpered, and Harris felt as if he should protect him from this humiliation, but he did want this information. A student's background, the traumas or fears that held them back could be very valuable to the teacher.

And, okay, as the two dads went on describing the antics of their toddler, how each day they tried and each day the same thing happened for a full two weeks, well it wasn't funny, but they told it that way.

"So in the end," James said, "we gave up and

decided he didn't want to learn to swim. Probably would avoid any body of water bigger than the bathtub for the rest of his life."

"You never tried again, when he was older?"

Stephen shook his head. "We talked about it, but were afraid we'd already scarred him for life." His merriment gone now, he spoke low and serious. "I know he wanted to take some lessons, try to get past it while he was with David, but when he learned Luca couldn't swim, well, he wasn't nice about it."

I flicked a glance to the side to see a single tear running down my omega's face and once again wanted to go find his ex and make him pay. Instead, I lifted him from the chair and settled him on my lap then linked my arms around his waist. "Well, whatever happened in the past, your son is doing a great job learning now. We're even going to a pool party next week so he can enjoy his new skills."

The dads gave each other a look and then faced me. "Thank you for helping our son," James told me. "He's been telling us about you, but we feel much better now that we've met you and seen the two of you together."

"And enough sadness." Stephen leaned forward and filled glasses from the pitcher. "Lemonade all around?" He added vodka to two then arched a brow at me.

"Vodka, yes." Seemed like a great idea.

"Me, too, Dad," Luca chimed in.

But Stephen handed him a glass of plain lemonade. "I think you might not want any alcohol, Son. That is...unless you're sure you're not?"

"Not what?" he asked, but I knew.

And I knew. In only two weeks, we'd managed to create a life. I just didn't know how his dads could tell. Or why I was sure they were right.

Chapter Fifteen

Luca

I shifted in Harris' lap to face him better. "What is it that we know, and why can't I have a drink?"

The three men, my fathers and my mate chuckled heartily, but at what I was still clueless.

Harris pulled me against his chest and placed a kiss on the top of my head. "What your fathers are saying is that there's a chance you may be carrying my babe—our babe. It would probably be prudent not to take a chance. Lemonade only for you, okay?"

I looked to my fathers and then back at Harris. "Already?"

They cracked up even more and my father Stephen said, "It only takes once and with our genes inside you, there's probably been a lot more than once already."

"Dad!" I groaned and buried my face in Harris' chest. "See? I told you."

Harris rubbed my back and chuckled. "It's okay. It's a healthy thing to be open and honest about this stuff. Are you not happy, mate? About being pregnant or the possibility?"

I heard the slight change in his tone. I'd been worried about being embarrassed in front of my mate and had overlooked the elephant in the room.

Somehow I knew it was true. I'd had no nausea or anything of the sort, but call it gut instinct of the most puntastic nature.

I was pregnant.

With Harris' baby.

And he wasn't angry.

No, he seemed to be happy at the possibility.

I sat up and kissed Harris right on the lips. "I'm overjoyed that I have our child inside me, alpha. I couldn't have dreamed it would be so soon, but I'm happy. Are you?"

My chin quivered as I asked the question. He raised his thumb to calm my shaking. "I am the happiest man in the world. You have made it so, Luca."

My fathers hugged each other, and a few tears were shed.

Harris laughed. "Should I save the jokes about me having good swimmers 'cause I'm a swimmer for later or..."

Everyone in the room cracked up. My mate had officially won over my fathers just by his reaction to my pregnancy. I looked down at my belly, not really expecting anything, but simply knowing we had a life inside me, created by our love, was enough to make me warm all over.

James rose from his chair. "Enough of this sappy mess. I brought plenty of food to cook. How about pasta alfredo?"

The thought of my dad's comfort food made my stomach growl. "Yes, Dad. You make the best pasta."

He nodded and kissed my other dad on the temple. "Gotta feed the grandkid now."

"Grandkid?" I whispered more to myself than anyone else. This was all so new.

"I'm going to help him in the kitchen. Give you

two a moment of privacy."

Stephen, my other father, rubbed my back a little and then ruffled Harris' hair.

When he was gone, I couldn't help myself. I leaned down and kissed Harris. I ran my tongue along his lips, begging for entrance, and when he gave it to me willingly, a moan came from my mouth.

"Oh, omega mine, the things you do to me." His furrowed brow lessened and a soft smile played at the corner of his mouth. "We're going to have a family."

At the sound of the word family coming from his lips, in that context, a lone tear welled in my eye. "Is that okay?"

You know, just in case that whole sweetest thing anyone has ever said to me was fake for my fathers.

Which I knew Harris wouldn't do.

But I was who I was and needed the reassurance of my alpha. I probably would for quite some time until my knowledge of my mate superseded my fear of David.

"It's more than okay, Luca. I meant what I said. You have made me the luckiest man in the world. I have your love in my heart and my babe in your belly. What more could I possibly ask for? You've made me complete."

I needed his embrace in that moment and he didn't keep it from me. Harris pulled me to him and tucked my head into the crook between his shoulder and neck. He rubbed my back and said all the simple but boundless ways that he loved me and how we would be happy as a family.

I had a family of my own now.

The thought was empowering and terrifying all at once.

I inhaled deeply, taking in the scent of my male, now mixed with the smells of garlic, butter, and cream coming from the kitchen where my fathers were cooking.

"Let's go join them before I take you to your bedroom and really embarrass you, omega mine."

I shifted a little and found that my mate's cock had grown hard while we cuddled.

I pulled back. "We were having a sweet moment." I kissed his nose.

He shrugged. "We were—we still are. But then you moved those hips a little and moaned into my neck. I can't help it, omega. I'll never get enough of you."

I chuckled and put my hand to my belly. His eyes grew wide and he mimicked my motion, covering my hand with his. "I bet you will when I get huge."

The intensity in his stare told me otherwise. "No, omega mine. You might find the opposite to be true. Because the thought of you, rounded with our babe inside you, well..."

He moved my hand to graze against his groin and found his dick harder than it had been before, and I didn't know that was even possible.

Pregnancy might have its perks, you know, other than giving us a child.

"I love you, alpha. You've given me hope for life."

He tugged me in for one searing kiss before getting up. "And you, Luca, have given me everything in return. Let's go. My resolve is getting thin."

Chapter Sixteen

Harris

We spent the rest of the weekend together. I wasn't sure I should with James and Stephen staying, but they seemed so sure I was staying that I went along with it. Just swore to myself we wouldn't be doing anything likely to raise the dead, or the dads as the case might be.

And I held firm until we arrived in the bedroom and the door clicked closed behind us.

I headed into the adjoining bathroom where Luca promised me a spare toothbrush could be found and cleaned up a bit, stripped down to my boxers for comfy sleeping. But when I returned, I found my omega naked on top of the blue denim quilt, sprawled and sexy, dick jutting into the air, and knees spread to give me a view of the crinkled entrance to paradise. I froze, swallowing past the huge lump in my throat. I'd never seen anyone so beautiful. My eyes filled with tears at his flat stomach, soon to swell with our child.

"You'd...you'd better get under the covers before you catch a cold, omega," I choked out as my cock got the message and tented my white cotton boxers.

He reached down and closed his fist around his meaty cock, rubbing up and down, smearing the precum over its length. His broad smile told me he knew exactly the effect he had on me. "Do I look cold, alpha?"

Sassy omega.

"Well, your nipples are pretty stiff."

He pulled his legs close to his body and wider apart. "Do you really think that's from cold?" His fist never eased its steady strokes as he spoke. "Because I don't believe that's the case."

I moved again, my feet shuffling me forward toward the side of the bed where I came to a halt, nostrils flaring at the scent of his arousal. "And do you have a theory?" I watched him jerk off, hardly able to breathe. "Maybe something I can do about that?"

His eyes drifted halfway closed. "Mmm...I'm open to all suggestions."

I heard soft voices from the wall behind the bed and glanced at Luca, startled. "Is that? Oh god, no. We can't possibly..."

"We can't possibly not, alpha. I need you."

And of course that word triggered all alpha things inside me. Alphas must care for their omegas. It was my primary impetus. I wanted to feed him and our child, clothe them, provide for them, fulfill every one of their needs and desires. And right now, Luca was asking me to do that.

Still, I hesitated. "What about your dads? What will they think?"

His lips twitched. "I already told you what they put me through. Turnabout is fair play."

I cleared my throat. "Umm..." I wasn't sure it worked that way. Still, my jerking, aching dick was pointed in the direction of my desires like a divining rod. I had the vaguest idea it might take off on its own if I didn't act. Okay, ridiculous, but when all your blood has headed for your groin, it's awfully hard to think clearly. "We have to be quiet."

But he threw his head back, panting, and I had no more willpower left. My alpha overwhelmed my future son-in-law desire to make a good impression. Grasping his wrist, I stilled his movements. "I believe that's my job, omega."

The liquid gaze he turned toward me, the labored breaths, his hips still rising and falling although he was no longer stroking himself... I'd never seen anything so hot in my life. "Then do your job, alpha."

Continuing to hold his wrist, with the vague idea of making sure he didn't suddenly make himself come, I managed to struggle out of my boxers past the stiffened member making it difficult, I flung myself at his side and, finally releasing his arm, gathered him in my arms. He faced me, and I lifted his top leg over my body and braced it on my hip. "That's right, just there," I muttered before pressing my lips to his, tasting him, the rough denim of the comforter beneath us adding one more sensation. His skin was warm, the light covering of hair scraping my ultra-sensitized skin. We had no light on in the room, but the bathroom fixture still sent enough of a glow for me to take in everything I needed to.

I cupped his cheek and tilted his head, deepening the kiss, tangling tongues with him, tasting what I already knew. His body chemistry had already altered, letting me know, as if I hadn't already been aware that he carried our child. This time next year there'd be a crib by our bed, but for now it was just us, me and my omega, celebrating the most wonderful night of our life together so far.

I lifted my head to get a breath. "He's going to be just like you," I murmured, taking a lick at his throat. "Too good-looking for his own good."

"Uh-uh," he replied. "She will be like you, strong and kind and incredible looking."

"She?" I'd been picturing a miniature version of my omega. "Okay, whatever you want."

"Silly alpha." He groaned as I brought my lips to his masculine nipples, licking them to even tighter peaks. "The baby is what it is. We can't control that."

"Then we need a unisex name, one that works for either." I suckled the other nipple, my fingers creeping down to close around his cock. "Like Sam or Jamie."

He shuddered. "Can't we wait to name the baby until we are far enough along to know the sex? There's no rush. It's probably the size of a grain of rice or something. Even he or she may not know the sex it plans to be yet."

Was that how it worked? But I was adamant. "Nope, we can't call it nothing, like it's a stranger. Members of the family need a name."

We got distracted then as I positioned myself between those spread legs and pressed my cock inside his tight ring. Had a man ever been this tight? I worked my way inside, the rippling muscles of his tight passage taking me higher, faster than I'd ever climbed before. I plunged in and retreated, over and over, holding back as best I could, but when he closed his fist around his cock again and gave a squeeze, sending spurts of creamy cum over his belly, my mind blew along with my dick.

I poured my cum into him, the added heat sending

him into another mini orgasm, something else I hadn't known was possible, but the creamy trail rolling down his cock could not be denied.

I dropped over him, bracing myself on my forearms for a few minutes of panting until a bang on the wall startled me and I landed on my omega.

"Oof!"

I scrambled off him. "Are you all right?" I stared at his belly as if I could see any damage caused by my clumsiness.

"Fine." But he rolled his eyes. "Yeah, Dad?"

My cheeks burned as I tried to think how noisy we might have been, what they could have heard.

"Alex is a good name for a boy or a girl," one of the dads said. The wall muffled the sound enough I couldn't tell which. "After your grandfather."

Yeah, they heard everything.

But it was kind of a good name.

Chapter Seventeen

Luca

I enjoyed my dads being around, I did, but they left after only a week, citing the fact that Harris and I needed some real alone time.

You know, without anyone listening through the walls.

"Tomorrow is the day," Harris said as I came up from another holding-my-breath-under-the-water session. At this point in my lessons, I could float, kick, and dog paddle like a pro—maybe even save myself from drowning, but I looked forward to the real swimming, like my mate did.

"It is. I got new swim shorts and everything."

There was no one in the pool with us. The kids had gone for the evening, and he knew Edison and George were gone as well. The pool around me was lit by large yellow lights underneath the water.

Harris looked at me, and then down to my belly. "I wanted to talk to you about something and have you not be scared."

My stomach sank.

"What?" I asked, and my voice cracked.

"Come here, omega mine." He held his hands out and I held on to the sides of the pool and worked my way to him.

"Tell me."

He cleared his throat. "I wanted to know...and I know it's soon and all but, can we move in together? I can't stand the nights when we can't be together. I want to wake up with you every morning."

The past few weeks had been weird. I spent the night at home a lot since my dads were there, and Harris went home for laundry and things like that. One or two times, he decided to stay home and sleep. We'd actually missed that pool party that had initially been going to be our first date. We might have had other stuff going on.

Because we got no sleep together. And Edison and Liam understood perfectly, albeit with lots of teasing.

"Can we move into my place?"

I realized moving into my place was my own defense mechanism. If something happened, I could kick him out.

How horrible of me to think that way.

He nodded and smiled at me like I'd given him a gift. "Your place is bigger. Is that a yes? I want my family together."

His hand was on my belly now, and warmth began to flow up my legs and to all the places.

Trust—I had to trust.

"That's a yes. I don't want to be apart from you, either."

He kissed me long and hard right there in the pool. "Now, do you think you can go all the way to the bottom? I'll go with you."

Harris wanted me not to be afraid of the bottom of the pool, which was a real issue for me.

"Not today. I'm actually exhausted," I said, making my legs churn under the water though sleepiness was taking over.

His eyes widened. "I'm so sorry. We've been here two hours. No wonder you're tired. What kind of alpha am I?" I heard the panic in his voice.

"Hey, I'm fine. All this human growing has me more tired lately. It's okay."

I risked letting go of the side to touch his face.

"Let's go. Can we stop by my house so I can grab a bag of stuff, or do you need to go straight home?"

I made my way out of the pool after him. "That's fine. Also, I'm starving at the same time. This pregnancy thing is already fun."

He chuckled and pressed me against the swimming area wall. "It's going to be amazing. That's why I need to be with you. I don't want to miss a single thing."

Harris' blue eyes did me in every time. "I want you there—all the time."

He reached behind me and grabbed my ass. "Let's go. Food and bed for my lovely mate. And tomorrow, pool party."

After stopping for Harris' stuff and some Chinese takeout on the way home, I was beat. A hot bath sounded fantastic.

"Why don't I run you one, then. Can't be too hot though. That's what the pregnancy book says."

I looked at him as we went into the front door. "Did I say that aloud?"

He laughed and took my bag. "Yes, you did. I'm happy to oblige."

I slumped my shoulders. "But I'm starving at the same time."

He pulled me to lean on him. "No one says you

can't have General Tso's chicken in the tub. In fact, new rule. My mate can eat in the tub anytime he wants. Sit down while I run your bath and get you a plate made. I'm spoiling you rotten tonight."

I sat on the nearest flat surface and watched my mate go to work—on me. He ran water in the tub and then while it was filling, fixed a plate of Chinese and poured me a big glass of lemonade. He set both on the counter and then came to get me.

I knew Harris was strong, but when he lifted me up and carried me to the tub, I realized how strong.

He would never let me down.

I'd finally found the mate I was supposed to have.

"Let's get these clothes off," he murmured and kissed my neck before stripping me down. I hadn't the energy to do anything but let him. This baby baking took it out of a guy. "One foot at a time. Lean on me," he whispered.

"Can I always lean on you?" I asked in a sort of sleepy stupor.

"We can always lean on each other, Luca. I'm your rock, and you are mine. That's the way it's supposed to work." I slipped into the warm water and groaned. "I'll be right back, omega."

He came back with not only my plate, but the TV tray and all of the Chinese we'd ordered.

"What's happening?" I asked.

"I'm bathing with my love and feeding him dinner. That's what."

Chapter Eighteen

Harris

I sat on the closed toilet cover and watched my
mate drowse in the tub. He'd eaten every bit of the
General Tso's, the chow mein, and the Chinese long
beans he'd developed a passion for recently. His
midhusband said cravings were mostly in the mind of
the omega, but I didn't care where they came from. If
he had one, I made sure it was handled. As a result,
we'd eaten long beans twice today. If he desired them,
we'd have them for breakfast, too, but not until the
restaurant opened because we wouldn't have any left.

I made a mental note to see if we couldn't find
some at the farmer's market on Sunday. If we sautéed
them at home, we could control the salt, something I'd
read we should do while he carried my child.

The conventional wisdom as well as that provided
by his midhusband and every one of our friends
weighed heavy on me. I read every volume I could find,
studied one even now, and had come to the conclusion
that pregnancy was a long and terrifying road with
more possible dangers than the Canadian ice roads
those truckers drove on TV. So many ways to endanger
both my omega and our babe if we didn't do everything
just right. Even swimming at the pool. I read dozens of
articles about the benefits of the exercise, the comfort
a growing omega could find floating in the warm
water, before finding one that questioned its safety
based on the chemicals used therein.

And all of those things were merely what it took to get the omega to the delivery room where the real dangers began. I'd barely met Luca and already had helped him plummet into one of the most death-defying moments of his life. Why hadn't I waited? We didn't need to have a baby so soon...

My heart thudded in my ears as I imagined everything my web searches had told me could go wrong. The multiple horror stories told by others about their disastrous deliveries.

What if the baby didn't make it?

What if Luca didn't?

How could I have been so irresponsible as to impregnate him before we researched everything, learned what to do, how to maximize our chances of his coming through alive.

"Alpha?" His concerned voice cut through my frantic musings, and I jumped. "Are you feeling all right?"

While I'd been focused inward, my pregnant omega had climbed out of the tub, wrapped up in a towel, and set his tray on the side of the sink. He'd walked right up to me, and I hadn't even seen him coming. I'd thought I was watching over him, but clearly had not been.

What if he'd fallen? My breathing, already harsh, became shallow, and I dropped my head to my lap in an attempt to quell my hyperventilation before I passed out and made the situation even worse.

"Harris?"

Shit. What kind of an alpha went off the deep end this way?

"Harris!" His hand landed on my arm, grip tightening. "What's wrong? Are you sick?"

I probably looked charming, hunched over on the toilet like this. But my position was helping, and my breathing eased enough for me to straighten and offer him a weak smile. "No. I'm fine. Let's get you to bed."

He allowed me to stand, but then instead of my helping him from the room, he slung an arm around my waist and urged me into the bedroom. Honestly, I didn't have the strength to argue, and within a few moments he had me stripped to my boxers and tucked under the covers. Dropping his towel, Luca joined me, snuggling close and resting his head on my shoulder.

We lay there a few minutes, his thigh over my legs, the only light that the bathroom cast over the floor across the room. Despite my mind's inclination to take me to frightening places, our embrace calmed me, and reminded me of my duty to reassure, to protect, to deal with the situation as it stood rather than allowing the fears of what might happen to shut me down and make it impossible to care for my omega.

For now, I would feed him, protect him, make sure he attended his appointments with the midhusband. See to it that he had everything he needed and anything he wanted that was good for him. For example, yes on the sliced apples, no on the six chocolate doughnuts I'd caught him with the day before. One, yes. Two, no.

I calmed a bit more, but the possibilities for disaster still lurked, a dark cloud over my head, threatening to rain mayhem at any time.

"Okay, alpha, where are you?" This time, his voice

didn't startle me, it rolled over me like a soft, curling wave. And his body pressed to mine added to the effect.

"Don't worry, Luca, just thinking."

He lifted his head and met my gaze in the dimness, his eyes holding so much wisdom I knew he'd never believe a platitude. So I was honest. "Pregnancy is a serious matter." Honest, but minimal.

"Mmm hmmm." He sat up, the covers pooling at his waist, showing his very distracting toned chest. "What you mean is dangerous, right?"

"No, not...exactly."

"Exactly, alpha. I've seen your shelves filling with books, and I've gotten up a couple of times when I missed your warm bod in bed next to me to see you sitting in the living room at the computer. Now, either you are cheating on me?" He raised an eyebrow.

"Of course not!" He couldn't believe that.

"Taking a night class in underwater basket weaving?"

"No." Yeah, he was onto me.

Luca cupped my cheek and gave me a soft smile that melted me from my toes on up. "Then you're looking at all the things that can go wrong in a pregnancy. Didn't you know that's the number one mistake pregnant dads and their alphas make?"

"It is?" I blinked. "But what—"

He pressed a soft kiss to my lips. "We have a great midhusband and one solid book he recommended. Let's use those resources instead of reading the pregnancy version of pulp novels. Sure, things go wrong, but we're doing everything right. You are helping me watch my diet, we're exercising in the pool, I take the supplements, and visit my practitioner. Etc. etc." Another kiss, this one deeper and one I took control of for a long moment before we surfaced for it and spooned, exhausted. At least I was, and he needed as much rest as possible to grow our baby.

As the fog of sleep swirled into my brain, I struggled free to ask one question. "How do you know my research was the number one mistake?"

"I found it in a list called *Top Ten Pregnancy Goofs*."

"We're two of a kind, omega." His soft laugh followed me into sleep.

Chapter Nineteen

Luca

"I'm not. You can forget it." I caught a glimpse of myself in the mirror at the My Brother, My Sister club locker room and right then threw my damned swimming trunks in the trash—never to surface again.

Harris sighed, and I could see him screw his mouth up right and left trying not to smile. "But we both agreed continued exercise was good for you."

"Don't you laugh at me, Harris. You did this."

We both lost our ability to be serious. I was pacing back and forth, trying to accept the fact that I was no longer cute in my swimming trunks.

In fact, I looked like I'd gone to the beach and had swallowed the beach ball.

"*We* did this." He walked over to me and stroked my belly, which was now big as all get-out. "And I happen to think you are lovely, omega mine."

"Don't try to butter me up. Literally, no butter anymore. I've probably gained fifty pounds. If I tried to get in the pool, it wouldn't matter if I could swim or not. I'd simply float. Fat floats."

Harris rolled his eyes. "You are carrying our babe. It takes up some stomach room. I know. Hard to believe. And the midhusband says you've only gained about ten pounds. All of that is baby. Don't tell me you're not excited to have a little Luca running around making trouble."

I blew out a breath and centered myself. Of course, I was excited and happy.

It was a shock to see myself this big.

And only seven months along.

I still had two months more to grow.

I would pop like a balloon, I just knew it.

"I am. I promise I am." I blew out a weighted breath. "Can we do something fun?"

Harris beamed. Fun was practically his middle name but lately I hadn't been up to it.

"I think I have just the thing."

In less than a half hour, we were at the mall. Not exactly my idea of fun.

"This is the place you wanted to go?"

He smiled again and took my hand. "I've been wanting to baby shop, but we haven't had much time. Wanna buy a bed for our babe?"

Then he winked at me, and the last thing I wanted to do was be in a public place.

"That actually sounds amazing."

"I love you, Luca. In case I haven't said that lately." Then he kissed me until I couldn't think straight.

We found the perfect crib right away. It would transition to a toddler bed and then one day a single bed.

"Look at these, Luca."

I should've known my alpha wouldn't stop at a crib, and I had to admit, shopping for our little one made it all real.

Not that the kicking and huge belly didn't make it real.

Within the next hour, we had filled three huge shopping bags. The furniture would be delivered. I sat in the food court while Harris put the bags in the car.

He'd said he had one more thing in mind.

With my alpha, there was just no telling what that meant.

He returned with two tickets to the carousel and held out his hand. "Come on, love. One ride by ourselves before we two are three."

He acted like I was popping the baby out tomorrow.

With heated cheeks, I clambered onto the ride. We were the only ones riding on a weekday, so really no one could see us. We got into one of the sleigh-looking seats—I was so not getting on a horse—and he tugged my hand into his lap, linking our fingers.

The lights and borderline creepy music made me laugh, and Harris wrapped his arm around my shoulder. "Ah, love, that's my favorite sound in the world. After this ride, I'm ready to get you home...for another kind of ride."

I felt my eyebrow raise. "Oh really? Wow. Carousels do it for you. Who knew?"

He chuckled. "It's a surprise for me, too."

After he helped me down, we walked to the car. I leaned against the window and thought about how my life had changed in so little a span of time.

"What are you thinking about way over there?" Harris' voice interrupted my thoughts in the best way possible.

"How life is crazy," I said and looked at him. His hair had grown longer in the last couple of months and curled even more.

"How so?"

I shrugged. "I signed up for swimming lessons so I won't drown, but you made me realize I was drowning in more ways than water. You saved me when I was flailing in life and didn't even know it. You grounded me and gave me a family all in one package."

He wiped his face. "You did the same for me, except I wasn't drowning—I was floating around aimlessly. You're my anchor."

Well didn't that just put an arrow right through my heart.

"Get us home, alpha."

He ran his hand up my thigh. "Yes, sir."

Chapter Twenty

Harris

Truth, the past month or so our sex life had slowed a bit. My omega was wearing baggy T-shirts and pj pants to bed and could not be convinced I truly found him as enticing as ever, but for some reason our little excursion to the mall and ride on the carousel helped.

A lot.

When we got home, he dragged me up the walk to the door and began to strip the moment it closed behind us. I watched in wonder at the change in his demeanor. And appreciation at the changes our babe had wrought within his body. All his gain was in the bump that protruded straight out from his middle. So far, he didn't seem to have the bloating problems the midhusband had warned us to watch for. No, he looked like the same hunky omega I'd first made love to, with the added attraction of carrying our child.

"Well?" he demanded, hands on hips, naked and proud in the middle of the living room. "Are you going to join me?"

"Oh, hell yes." I followed him into the bedroom, dropping my clothes as I went, so by the time I arrived at the bed, we were both ready for anything. "Looks like the carousel did it for you, too, omega," I crooned, easing him down onto the edge and dropping to my knees.

"You do it for me, alpha." He sucked in a breath

when I closed my fist around his proud erection and, pausing to kiss his abdomen, drew it toward my parted lips. "I just needed to make sure I still did it for you."

Why had he ever doubted?

But we had lots of time to talk, and at the moment I wanted to show him my feelings about his body by worshiping it. I'd also love to do it inch by inch—all of it—but concern for his energy level, especially after such a long, emotional day, convinced me to go for the gusto.

Or the blow job, as the case might be.

Flicking a glance upward, I saw his cheeks flush, pupils dilate, and the tip of his tongue swipe his lips. Oh yeah, all good signs. In the recent past, I hadn't seen most of them, as if he'd held a bit of himself back.

My lips closed around the tip of his dick, and his hands planted on my shoulders. Fingers tightening and releasing in sync with my glides down and up his cock, taking more with each descent. He tasted of salt and sweetness and that something extra that said he was a pregnant omega. An aphrodisiac unlike any other, almost a drug for me. Trancelike, I nibbled and licked, scraped my teeth over the shaft, and sucked on the head, slow, not speeding up no matter how he begged.

And he did.

I loved it.

When his breathing sped up, I cupped his sac and gave it a gentle squeeze. Luca shrieked and his cum poured into my mouth, down my throat where his tip already dwelled, and lifted my arousal to the point I had a flash of wondering whether I could come just from his cum.

He flopped back on the bed, panting, and I let his half-erect dick slip from my mouth. "My turn, omega." I hesitated, although my cock twitched against his calf. "If you're up for it?"

He nodded, his eyes half-closed. "Always, my love."

"I love you, omega." I rose to my feet and tugged his ass closer to the edge of the bed, folded his legs back over his chest to reveal his slick and his hole. Paradise. "You are so ready for me, aren't you?" I glided a finger over the slipperiness then inside, amazed that no matter how often I'd taken him, he was always tight around even a single finger. I replaced the finger with my cock and, with a single push, breached him, my head engulfed by his body.

Pausing there, I savored the welcome his body offered before moving deeper, a fraction of an inch at a time, my legs trembling with the effort not to thrust all the way in. I retreated and pushed forward, once, twice, three times before he stirred restlessly. "More, alpha. I need all of you."

No further invitation needed, I did as he asked. I drove all the way home. My balls slapped the globes of his magnificent ass with each plunge. "I...don't...think this is going to last long," I told him, glancing down to see his cock once again proud and ready...so soon. How great had his need been? "Touch yourself, omega. I want to see you jerk off and come with me."

His eyes opened wide, but his hand crept down to close around his dick and stroked. I held still for a long moment, using all my willpower not to come yet, wanting the moment to last watching him squeeze and release until, with a groan, he spurted all over my stomach and chest, the white cream dripping onto his torso. "Now, alpha, I want...ahhhh."

"I got you, omega." The sight had sent me, too, and my balls boiled, cum pouring into his welcoming body, the muscles gripping me inside until my knot started to grow. Not something that happened often, or usually during pregnancy, and I fell to the bed beside him, taking him to his side while we were bonded in that way.

I wouldn't have thought I could love him more, but I did. Our souls were as joined as our bodies, our child safe inside him until it grew enough to join us and sleep in that crib we'd bought today.

Love. Joy. Gratitude.

I fell asleep awash in those emotions, and in the embrace of the man I'd never dreamed I'd find. My perfect mate.

Chapter Twenty-One

Luca

"You can start the shower now. I brought the chocolate!" Liam, Edison's mate called out from the front door. Edison had decided to give Harris and me a baby shower here at my house—now our house. Harris had officially moved in, and his place had gone back up for lease.

"Oh, thanks. That's what I need—more calories." I rubbed circles in my round belly and everyone around chuckled.

Liam brought in chocolates and candies in all shapes and sizes. Gummy pacifiers, chocolate diapers, and even some white chocolate diaper pins.

And my fathers had gone way overboard on the cake as well.

We didn't know the gender of the baby yet and were still both on the fence about deciding if we would find out at all. The ultrasound was scheduled for next week.

Two months to go.

Two months and our little family of two would be three.

I'd gotten past the gross part and was coming into the nesting phase. We'd cleaned this house so many times over the past month, but it didn't stop me from dusting and vacuuming constantly. At least it was a little exercise.

That, plus the bedroom exercise.

Harris made sure we got plenty of that.

Okay, it was mostly me.

"You're still growing that babe. But yeah, that's a lot of sugar. Maybe just one." Harris picked up a heart-shaped chocolate and gently put it in my mouth.

The taste was divine—sweet and creamy. Liam could give Godiva a run for its money.

My house was decked out with pink and blue streamers along with balloons and with a huge bouquet Harris had brought in the day before.

He always bought me flowers on Sundays when he went out to get us coffee.

He made the bed every morning.

Our babe got a song from him every night.

My mate was the best.

"Well, the food is here. Let's get these presents opened!" Stephen, my dad, seemed to be the most excited about being a grandfather. He wanted to be called Padre.

He'd been watching too much *Daddy's Home*.

Harris escorted me to the chair marked with my name and balloons tied to the back. I opened the first gift, from Liam and Edison. It was several onesies with the overlapping shoulder flaps and little pants to match each one. All in yellow, of course, because gender not known.

I saved my fathers' gifts for last. They had each given us a box and also an envelope laid on the table.

Something in my gut told me they had gone overboard.

"Ours next," my other dad said and handed me a box.

I tore open the wrapping and inside was a nursing pillow and a car-seat cover. As soon as I cooed over the gift, another one took its place. Between our friends, we would have plenty to start this babe's life with.

That, plus our shopping trips.

"Another one, Dad?" I ripped open the paper to reveal a car seat. We needed another one. We'd purchased one, but needed one for each car. "Thanks, Dad!"

Then they handed me an envelope.

Inside was a picture of a home and my heart beat overtime. "What is this?"

My dads hugged each other around the shoulders. "Well, we couldn't exactly live so far from our grandkid, could we? We bought a home in the neighborhood. Hopefully, we can be a gift to you, being so close."

I jumped up and hugged them tightly. "I am so grateful!" And I was so appreciative. Harris and I were clueless. We could use more hands around, and their child-rearing experience.

It was so different this time. David had wanted to move away from my family, but now as Harris embraced them both and thanked them, I knew my life was leaps and bounds better.

After another hour or so, people began to file out, filled to the brim with cake and candies and other goodies my fathers had cooked up. They had decided to stay at a hotel while their things were delivered and then they would move into the house.

We had the best family here. All of them had become our family in the past months.

"Finally," Harris murmured, wrapping his arms around my middle. "I've got you all to myself again."

I chuckled and leaned back into his hold. "Yes, you do. Today has worn me out."

We'd been up since early that morning, picking up the cake and decorating the house, not to mention, making it Luca-pregnant clean.

"I can't wait to see our babe next week. It seems like forever in the future."

I put my hands atop his. "Forever sounds great with you."

He kissed the side of my neck. "You say the sweetest things, omega mine."

"I mean every word."

Chapter Twenty-Two

Harris

Time was zipping past now, keeping us super busy. With so many milestones to keep track of, I wondered what I'd done with all my time before I had a mate and a baby on the way. And where we'd find the time to do everything once the baby arrived!

We had gotten the baby shower gifts put away— barely—when the ultrasound day arrived. Still going back and forth on whether we were anticipating the arrival of a little boy or girl. I was still voting for a birth day surprise, but my oh-so-practical omega, he who was chasing down any dust bunny or bit of lint that dared enter his nest, wanted to know.

"People only started this blue and pink thing a hundred years ago, or maybe two hundred...but historically babies were dressed alike," I reminded him.

"I don't care about that anyway."

Since we had a dresser full of yellow already, we would be adding other colors we liked to suit us rather than society's expectations. "Then why can't you wait?" I held his car door open while he waddled up and settled in his seat.

He tipped his face up at me, the sun shining on his flushed cheeks and sparkling eyes. "I just want to know everything about this baby. Are they well? Everything okay? And their name. Don't you want to know their name?"

Struck dumb, I bent for a quick kiss then closed the door and went around to climb in. Not that I'd say the baby hadn't been a person for me until now, but this was a whole new way of thinking about them.

Silence stretched between us as we drove toward the center of town, but then I pulled into an open spot on the street.

"What's wrong?" Luca asked. "Are we out of gas or something?"

I turned and took his hands in mine, shaken to my core with the realization that the baby was coming very soon. That their sex was something already determined, every bit of their body formed. We hoped they'd hold out on their arrival until their due date, or close to it, but at just short of seven and a half months' gestation, they were big enough to survive if they put in an early appearance.

Our baby was a whole person in there, just finishing up their preparations for joining us. I could picture the little one, imagine holding them, kissing their petal-soft cheek. Tears flooded my eyes and I lifted his hands and kissed each finger. "I'm so grateful to you," I choked out. "You are making us a baby, making us a family. I'll never be able to repay you."

His lips quirked, one corner lifting, but his eyes were shiny, too. "I didn't do it by myself, you know. I should be thanking you." He shook his head. "But if you want to do something for me...?"

"Anything, omega." A tear dripped off my chin. "Just tell me what you want."

"I want to know the sex."

Duh. I'd gotten so emotional, my brain had shut

down. But... "So do I. I want to know everything about this baby." I hesitated. "But let's not find out today."

He blinked. "So you don't want to know the sex?"

"I found a place that does 4-D images. I held back because I knew it would show everything, but they have an opening later today. Let me make a call and we can head over there instead. The midhusband in fact recommended a facility he trusts."

He frowned. "Our insurance won't cover that, will it?"

"Nope, but you aren't to worry about that. It's my gift to you, and not as expensive as yours. To us. Unless you don't want to?"

His smile told me everything I needed to know, and a few minutes and two phone calls later we were on our way to the imaging center located in Violetville, two hours away.

I scooted around the car and helped Luca out, as had become my habit despite any protests on his part, but this time he groaned as he stood. "That was too long a drive for this omega," he said, a hand pressed to his back. Then he grinned and patted his belly. "Only for the opportunity to get a good gander at you, babyface."

The single-story building had obviously been a home once, and the business owners had managed to keep the cottage charm with window boxes full of violets and low shrubbery lining the path to a porch featuring a pair of white wooden rockers. But inside it was all about the tech. Once we signed in and I handed over my credit card, we were ushered to a room twice as large as our living room at home, furnished with, in addition to an exam table disguised to look more like a chaise lounge, two sofas and a huge wide-screen monitor that encompassed nearly an entire wall.

As we took in the environs, a woman dressed in a white lab coat bustled in pushing a cart holding various electronics I assumed would provide the images. "Welcome!" she chirped. "So you're here to get a peek at baby today. I assume since you are doing a 4-D moving image you don't mind knowing the sex?"

Luca cast me a glance before replying, "We can't wait to find out."

The procedure was similar to the 2-D ultrasound, and the tech explained each step as she went along, instructing me to have a seat while she got everything ready then, because I was obviously twitching to get closer to my omega, waving me back to his side.

"Ready?" She held the device above his jellied-belly and began moving it in circles. "Don't look at his tummy, look at the screen."

Across the room, on the giant monitor, a little face emerged.

"She's smiling," Luca whispered, reaching out as if he could touch her on the screen.

"So beautiful," I breathed.

"Let's see more and determine if you're right." The tech made more motions then nodded. "Yep, she's a girl. And active!"

We held hands while our beautiful, exquisite genius of a daughter brought her tiny hands to her mouth as if blowing kisses, pouted her lips, and moved about in her safe, warm world. All too soon the session was over, and I would never be the same again.

"Madelyn?" Luca asked, while the tech wiped his belly clean.

"Yeah," I kissed him then straightened. "That's our Maddie."

Chapter Twenty-Three

Luca

Swimming lessons had halted for me as my due date approached, but I went to the pool from time to time, simply to relax and watch as my alpha taught the kids at the center. I waded in the shallows, not because I couldn't swim, but because no one wanted to see a prego man floating belly-up like a whale ready to be harpooned—no one.

That morning, I'd been more wound up than ever and really needed the distraction. After an hour, I felt more relaxed. Carrying a babe sure was work. I hadn't been able to get much done, paying job-wise in a few months. We had plenty in savings and watched our pennies, so it wasn't that big a deal.

Still, I felt stressed and was at the point where I wanted this babe out of me.

I was two weeks past due after all.

Water sloshed around my legs as I got out of the pool. I had to hold onto the rail like the elderly people did who swam here on Sunday afternoons.

"You're getting out? Let me help you." Harris had Michael Phelps-style swum over to me and stopped beside me.

"I'm good. Go back to your students," I said and blew him a kiss. I went from the pool area to the locker room with steady and slow footsteps. The last thing I wanted to do this large was to slip and fall and break my ass.

Might put me into labor though.

I stripped in the shower stall and let the warm water wash off all of the chlorine.

I needed a nap—again. Second one that day.

As I turned off the water, I felt some pressure and then, out of nowhere, my water broke, right there in the shower.

"Huh, convenient."

I was unnervingly calm about the whole thing.

I rinsed off one more time, careful to note any contractions of which there were none. I toweled off and got dressed, grabbed my bag, and went to see Harris.

"Hey, Harris!" I called out from the side of the pool. He swam over with a smile on his face.

"What, my love?"

"Are you about done?"

He chuckled and looked back at his group. "Yeah, we're just playing around."

"Okay, because, um, my water just broke in the shower and..." A ripple of pain took over my back, and I grabbed onto the ladder next to me for both balance and, you know, not falling into the pool mid-contraction.

"Everyone out of the pool!" Harris shouted, and I grabbed my chest. He'd scared the crap out of me. He scrambled out, took my bag from me, and spoke in hushed tones, trying to be calm, and failing. "Let's get you to the hospital."

I nodded while he called Gary who said he would meet us at the hospital. He ushered me into the car and I breathed, holding his hand on the way.

"Can you step on it? This babe is coming—now!"

I raised up my bottom, trying to ease the onslaught of pain, but nothing helped.

"Okay. Two minutes, Luca. Two minutes, I swear."

We pulled into the hospital and I got out before Harris could get around to my side. Tim, my midhusband, was there, waiting with a wheelchair. "We don't have a lot of time." I groaned and held tight to Harris' wrist.

"You're sure?" Gary asked.

"I'm couldn't be more sure. Get me to a room."

I barely made it to the hospital room where I leaned over the couch for visitors, and with Harris' hands in my hair and Gary waiting behind me, pushed out our babe.

Two pushes, that's all it took.

"Oh, there's Daddy's Madelyn," Harris cooed as Gary showed her to us and then took her for cleaning up and weighing—all the newborn things.

"She's gorgeous," I proudly told Harris. She has his curls, that was what I saw first.

"Just like her papa. You did so well. I was scared to death but you..."

I teared up at his praise. Madeline was presented to us with a white blanket and sleeping. She was too perfect—almost like a doll.

"Now you are a family," Gary said. "I'll be outside for a minute—give you two a moment alone with your daughter."

We nodded and Harris took the babe while I cleaned up and got into the bed.

He handed her to me and she went straight for the milk.

My life had turned out just the way I wanted.

Epilogue

Harris

I always wanted my own pool, although I'd never told a soul. They were expensive and everyone said they didn't make back the investment when you sold the house, so impractical as well. But I'd dreamed of one since I was a kid.

And my own omega.

And a family.

Luca made it all happen. Six months after he brought our daughter into the world, we had a pool-warming party. Turned out that while he was waiting for our little lady to make her appearance, my omega had been making the arrangements. Construction didn't begin right away since his design required some hard work by our contractor to get the permits in line, but it was so worth it.

The lessons that began at the center continued there, and I finally had the chance to witness my handsome omega at the pool party I'd promised he'd enjoy. With one difference. The party was at our house.

Guests had been coming for an hour, bringing potluck dishes to contribute to the feast, and I'd been in the kitchen coordinating their storage for the couple of hours before we ate. Outside the window, a couple of dozen people mingled, nibbling on chips and nuts and enjoying the tropical drinks being blended up by my omega's dad. Warm sunshine sparkled on the turquoise waters. They felt the umbrella topped beverages went well with the incredible foliage around the rock-edged pool.

As soon as I got outside, I planned to get hold of one of those drinks myself and get into the swing of things. Madelyn floated in her little pool seat, safely in the hands of her proud papa, who seemed to love the pool almost as much as me. She was already taking swimming lessons and could blow bubbles with the best of them. Our little mermaid.

The trickle of arrivals waned, and I shoved a big bowl of potato salad into the crammed fridge and headed for the outside bar. While I'd been distracted, Luca had passed our daughter off to his dads, and she hung in her little sling on James' chest, eyes half-closed in the drowse of a happy, sun- and water-soaked baby. Her lashes fluttered a bit as she fought sleep as she did whenever there was something interesting going on.

"I'll have a mai tai," I told Stephen, casting a glance around. "Any idea where your son is?"

I couldn't make out what he was saying, the roar of the blender making margaritas or something drowning him out, but then he pointed and I turned to see a sight I'd never have thought possible a year and a half ago.

"He's on the diving board," I murmured in awe. And maybe a little bit of panic. "Is he okay? He can't dive."

James came around the bar and stood next to me, still supporting our daughter, Stephen on the other side. Together we watched Luca walk to the end of the board and pause. For a moment I thought to go save him, to stop him before he got hurt, but rather than freezing, he glanced in my direction and flashed a smile, gave a little bounce, and grabbed his legs as he leapt in the air and grasped his legs tight to his chest.

The resulting splash, the inevitable scuttle of guests away from the pool's edge with an array of colorful curses...led to laughter and, at least in my mind—admiration. As for me, I stood there with a huge lump in my throat and teary eyes.

Cannonball. He did a cannonball. My omega who was too afraid to wet his feet when I met him had managed that most obnoxious of childhood pool stunts. I shook my head with a sigh, watching the guests close in around him again, patting him on the back and congratulating him on his splash height.

I moved toward the pool and mounted the diving board as well, my last thought before following him into the water with a cannonball of my own that we were now a swimming family. In the pool as well as through life.

Our daughter was destined for the Olympics. We were sure of it. And of each other. And of our love.

Book 1 in the Theta-Mine Series

You've never seen an omega like this.

Max travels the world as a professional YouTuber, trying out candy shops and reviewing them online. He sometimes dates, sure, but as a theta, a different and unique kind of omega, he has to be careful about whom he connects with.

When he meets alphas Harry and Kian, his theta instincts know right away that they are *the ones*, but he has to wonder—do they know what that means for their future?

Harry and Kian love each other unconditionally, and while they are living an amazing life together as a couple, sometimes it feels as if something—or maybe someone—is missing. When Max comes into The Bistro at midnight looking for a bite to eat, the connection is instantaneous—he is their third.

Coming Soon! Theta Tryst: Book 3 in the Theta-Mine Series

Also by Lorelei M. Hart

At the Christmas Inn, not all presents are wrapped in a bow.

Innkeeper alpha Miller and his mate Winston have a merry life in the town where Christmas rules. When the holiday season rolls around, people come from all over the country to enjoy both their hospitality and the wonder that is their town. Guests spend their days building snowman, decorating wreaths, caroling, enjoying romantic sleigh rides, and indulging in every kind of Christmas treat anyone can imagine. But when an emergency forces a cancellation at the inn, it opens up a room for a certain omega whose misfortunes have piled high lately.

Omega Klaus' life is on a downward trend starting with the death of his uncle, who raised him as his own. On the way back from the funeral, Klaus is on his way to a blue Christmas when he finds himself in the middle of a winter wonderland. A wonderland he might enjoy more if his car wasn't broken down, and his pockets nearly empty thanks to his mean-spirited and scroogy employer, who decided that was the perfect time to let him go.

When the towns kindly mechanic offers to find him a place to spend the night, Klaus has no choice but to agree. He is dropped off at The Christmas Inn where he finds himself confronted by two alphas his every instinct insists belong to him. But they're married to each other, and trouples are rare. Besides, even if they felt the same, what does he have to offer two handsome, successful men like them? He's broke, recently unemployed, and alone.

When it becomes apparent that all three feel the connection, it triggers heat in this guileless omega, and a night of passion ensues. In the morning, the heat is over...which can only mean one thing. A Christmas present is on the way in the form of their baby.

The Heat is On is a sweet with knotty heat non-shifter MMM Holiday Male Pregnancy Romance that takes place in a small Christmas wonderland.

My name is Damon. I keep busy with freelance photography and taking in foster kids. After all, having those kids in my home is the closest I'll ever come to a family—a fact I've accepted since I was a teenager. One car accident ended all of those dreams.

Dating is out for omegas like me, at least, I've made it my rule. An alpha craves an omega who can give him a family. And I'm just fine with my life. My work makes it possible for me to give the kids I take in lots of time, something they need and deserve. Most of them haven't had an easy life. And Robbie...my current foster child needs my love and care more than any of the others so far. I thought I had it all figured out, but meeting Patrick has thrown me for a loop.

Patrick deserves more than a lesser omega, a broken shell of who I should be. But I can't help myself. His searing looks plus that signature pumpkin spice scent demand I pay attention. Pursue him. See if there is a chance he could be mine.

Autumn brings with it cooler days, but with Patrick in my life, the nights only grow hotter.

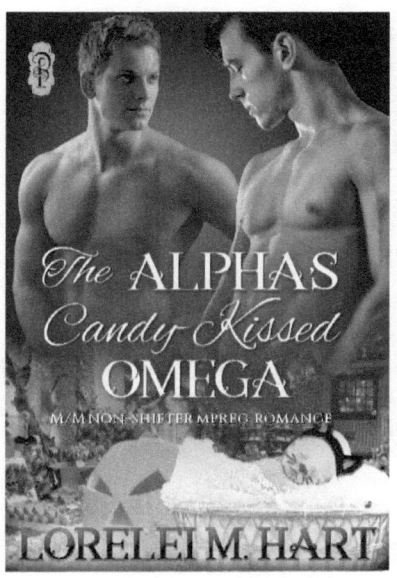

What better place to meet your fated mate than an extraordinary candy store?

And what better season than Halloween? Liam is arranging the amazing treats in the window of his gourmet candy shop, Sugar, when a jogger taps on the window. Despite his policy not to let strangers in when he's alone in the closed store, this stranger is too irresistible to send away.

Edison has had his eye on the hot alpha store owner for months but has finally gathered his courage to approach him. To his relief and delight, the man of his dreams asks him out on a date. Sweet!

But when a little boy who attends the afterschool activities at Edison's community center falls into desperate need, he is called upon to take him into his home and so a family begins. A foster child who has been so badly harmed brings challenges, and only a very strong, loving alpha would want to take on both an omega and the injured child. An unexpected pregnancy ups the ante.

They have found one another, but are things moving too fast? Can they take care of the children and each other as well as the businesses they are responsible for? Can they make a home?

The Alpha's Candy-Kissed Omega is a MM non-shifter mpreg with a hot successful alpha, a sexy, caring omega, a little boy who needs them both and an adorable baby. Plus a surprise or two along the way.

A long time ago, I met the alpha of my dreams.

We spent one night together, the most amazing of my life. He left me a note, but fate had other plans. I never knew his name, but he left me with something else— his babe in my stomach.

Now that my child and I have moved to a new town, I've found him again. But I have to tell him this boy is his son and hope he doesn't hate me.

All these years the only thing Bennett had of me was the first letter of my name and memories of that one night. But he has a son, so he must have a mate. I still love him, that fiery ginger from the rock concert. And I wonder why his son looks a little like me.

The Alpha's Lifeguard-Kissed Omega

About the Authors

Lorelei M. Hart is the cowriting team of USA Today Bestselling Authors Kate Richards and Ever Coming as well as Ophelia Heart, another bestselling author. Friends for years, the trio decided to come together and write one of their favorite guilty pleasures: Mpreg. There is something that just does it for them about smexy men who love each other enough to start a family together in a world where they can do it the old-fashioned way.